CAN'T FIND NOBODY

CAN'T FIND NOBODY

HOLLY JACOBS

Ilex Books 2016

ISBN-13: 978-0-9992736-9-2
ISBN-10: 0-9992736-9-8

Originally published as Found and Lost by
Harlequin Books
ISBN-10: 0373442009
ISBN-13: 978-0373442003

2004

Dear Reader,

Writing a book is like putting together a puzzle. You find a piece here and there, and eventually there's this eureka moment when you know you have a story.

I found the initial piece of this story back at Seneca High when Miss Mac made me student director for the play *Arsenic and Old Lace*. Next, there was a slight crush on actor Andrew McCarthy, which led me to watch *Weekend at Bernie's*. Then my editor told me I was killing off too many of my characters' relatives. "Dead people aren't funny, Holly." So I resurrected a few dead relatives, but really wanted to give her a very funny dead-body book ... and eureka! All the pieces were there and my story took form.

I had so much fun with this one, I hope you do as well!

Holly Jacobs

2016

PS. Wow, it's been twelve years since I wrote Markie's story. It was so much fun revisiting her. As you read her story, you'll note she doesn't have a cellphone at the beginning of the book. I know, it's hard to imagine now, but twelve years ago, a lot of people didn't. So much has changed since then for me as well. I've written a lot of books since Markie's story. More comedies, a lot of family dramas, and even another mystery series. Yes, Markie came before my bestselling Maid in LA Mysteries, but looking back, I think she pointed me in that direction. I hope you enjoy her story!

"Say that you found the body," Markie insisted, sounding unsure.

"I didn't. The neighborhood is pretty deserted this time of day," Zac replied.

"So now what?"

"We have no evidence a crime was ever committed. There is no body," he repeated.

"Sure there is. Somewhere. I tripped over it. Not that you care. Not that you ever cared."

Zac knew they were no longer talking about corpses, but were now talking about Joel. "Markie, that's not fair."

"Not fair is having a beautiful wedding with no groom because your supposed friend talked him out of marrying you."

"Listen, Markie—" He stopped short when his radio squawked with a request for him to return to the stationhouse ASAP.

"You'll be back to investigate my missing body?" she quizzed.

He hurried toward his car. "Nothing to investigate. No body, no crime. But I will be back to finish our discussion on just what I did and did not do at or before your wedding."

"My a/most-wedding. But *don't* bother," she hollered, then slammed her front door.

Nope, he sure hadn't missed her, but God, how he wanted her…

About the Author

Award-winning author Holly Jacobs has sold almost three million books worldwide. The first novel in her Everything But... series, *Everything But a Groom,* was named one of 2008's Best Romances by *Booklist,* and her books have been honored with countless other accolades.

Holly has a wide range of interests, from her love for writing to gardening and even basket weaving. She has delivered more than sixty author workshops and keynote speeches across the country. She lives in Erie, Pennsylvania, with her family and her dogs. She frequently sets stories in and around her hometown. You can visit the author online at www.HollyJacobs.com, or snailmail her at P.O. Box 11102, Erie, PA 16514-1102.

This one's for Kathryn,
who said dead bodies weren't funny.

And for Ethan, who said they were.

A special thanks to Erin Marquess, for helping with the
Philadelphia neighborhoods. Any errors are due to my own
directional inadequacies and not her superb descriptions!
To Matt, who knows real men buy romance. Thanks to
Katie and Abbey for the inspiration. Thanks to Lieutenant
DJ Fuhrmann, my own personal police resource, and to
Sharon Jann from the Philadelphia Police Department for
the Philly specifics! Finally, an apology to all emergency
dispatchers for poking fun at you … it was merely for
comedic effect. I totally respect the job you do every day!

An especially big thanks to a certain
dispatcher in Fairfax, Virginia!

Reviews

"Holly Jacobs' latest... is a delight. A darkly comic whodunit, it's her best book yet."
~RT BOOKclub

"Ms. Jacobs delivers a sweet love story filled with humor to enchant her readers... prepare to be thoroughly entertained
~Love Romances

"Holly Jacobs is the master of humorous writing."
~Writers Unlimited Reviewer

"Holly Jacobs hits the laugh track again with this fabulously funny tale of love and mystery."
~Romance Junkies

"...an exceptionally humorous and delightful tale."
~CataRomance Reviews

Contents

1

S plat!
   When Markie Walkowicz and her friends used to whack each other with snowballs during rare Philadelphia snowfalls, that's what it sounded like.

Splat, splat. They'd scream at the top of their lungs as snowballs whizzed back and forth.

It wasn't the fact that it was cold enough for snowballs that brought the word *splat* to Markie's mind on this particular Monday morning. It was the fact that the porch was rushing toward her face at an alarming rate.

Or rather, *she* was rushing toward the porch as she'd tripped and fallen.

Splat!

She landed hard in an inelegant heap. It took her a stunned moment to suck some frigid air into her rather deflated lungs.

It figured, she thought.

It just figured.

Markie was always more accident-prone when she was running late. And she was running so late this morning that she quickly decided a fast fall on the porch was better than the myriad of other accidents she might have attracted. Last time she was running this late, her front tire was flat.

She examined her throbbing knee, noting she had a hole in her stocking. She was going to have to go back in and change them, which meant she was going to be even later, but probably not as late as when she'd had to change that tire.

Panty hose might be torturous to put on, but they weren't nearly as difficult to manage as lug nuts.

Markie got up and immediately spotted what she'd tripped over.

It was a man.

A decidedly blue-looking man, laid out in front of her door.

A blue man wearing a green and orange plaid suit that was decades out of style.

"Mister?" she said, even though she instinctively knew she'd get no response.

The man's arm was thrown over his face. She reached out to touch his hand.

It was cold.

Markie screamed as she scrambled to her feet.

Screamed like a girl.

Loud, long and piercing.

Marquette Ann Walkowicz was the type of woman who prided herself on avoiding such feminine clichés as shrieking. She just didn't do it. Not about bugs, or even snakes.

No, Markie Walkowicz was not the type of woman who screamed like a girl.

But tripping over a dead body on the porch on a Monday morning when she was already late … well, that warranted a scream or two.

She stood for a moment, staring at the ugly plaid suit the dead man was wearing. It was so hideous that it was easy to focus on.

What to do?

What to do?

It was like trying to think through mud. Her brain had shut down as she stared at row after row of ugly pumpkin-orange and avocado-green plaid.

What to do?

It wasn't as if she had personal experience with discovering corpses on a front porch.

What to do?

She read a lot of women's magazines and they always had helpful hints on everything from hairstyles to how to please a man in bed, but she'd never seen an article about what to do when you trip over a dead body.

What to do?

What to do?

911.

Those three little numbers popped into her mind, glowing like some sanity-saving beacon.

She'd call 911 and they'd know what to do.

Markie did a ginger little leap over the body and into the house and then slammed the door.

Not only did she slam the door, she locked it, throwing the dead bolt and hooking up the chain.

After all, who knew how the man had died?

Maybe there was a murderer lurking in the bushes.

She rushed to close the front drapes and then ran to the phone. Her fingers were shaking as she punched those three numbers.

"911," the operator said. "What is the nature of your emergency?"

It took a second for her scream-strained vocal cords to respond to her command that they now produce a normal sound.

"There's a dead body on my porch," she finally managed in one quick burst.

"Your name?" the operator asked, no hint of shock or panic.

"Markie Walkowicz."

"And your address is?" the woman asked, continuing her calm questioning as if people called her all the time because they'd found bodies on their porches.

Markie had worked at a vast number of jobs over the years, but she was sure she'd never want a job where getting calls about corpses on the porch was par for the course.

"Ma'am, your address?" the operator asked again.

Markie told her.

"I've dispatched a unit," said Miss Calm-Cool-and-Collected. "Now, we'd better check the man—"

"*We'd?*" Markie interrupted, with a hint of a girl-scream back in her voice.

"—and feel for a pulse," the woman continued.

Purposefully, she forced herself to beat back her rising panic and speak in a usual tone. "You said *we* and by *we*, you mean me. You want *me* to go feel for a pulse. Sorry, ma'am, I'm not touching him again. There is no pulse. He's blue. And before you ask, there is no way I'm putting my lips on his for mouth-to-mouth. He's blue and cold. I don't need a medical degree to know that no amount of CPR is bringing him back."

There was a blue man in an orange and green plaid suit on her front porch.

As the realization sank in, Markie began to shiver uncontrollably.

There could be a murderer out there right now as well, peeking in the windows and watching her, deciding how he was going to kill her.

Feeling exposed, Markie took the phone and stepped into the coat closet.

She felt safer in its dark depths. Safer and just a bit warmer. The shivering slowed a bit.

"Did you recognize the man?" the operator asked, obviously having decided that she wasn't going to talk Markie into revisiting the body for either pulse-taking or CPR.

"I don't know. His hair was gray, so he was old. But his arm was sort of thrown up over his face so I didn't get a good look at him, and I wasn't moving his arm to get a better one. As a matter of fact, I don't know that I could move it. He felt sort of solid when I tripped over him."

"You tripped over him?" There was slight surprise in Miss Monotone's voice—the first hint of emotion she'd shown.

Markie had plenty emotion to spare, not that she could quite identify any one in particular. Her feelings were a mixed-up jangle at best.

"Yes, I tripped over him," Markie said. "He was right in front of my door, and it's Monday."

"Monday?"

"I was running late, and it's Monday, so I was in a hurry because I didn't want to spend the rest of the week trying to catch up. I have a meeting at the bank today, so I'm wearing business clothes instead of my normal jeans. I haven't even had a cup of coffee."

The fact that she was dealing with a corpse before coffee just seemed to make the situation worse. "Anyway, I was hurrying out and there he was … so I fell right over him and put a hole in my nylons."

"I see," Miss Armchair-Psychiatrist said.

I see. That's all she said, but Markie could hear a sort of a soothing quality in her voice, as if she were trying to calm a lunatic.

"I'm not crazy," Markie said.

"I didn't say you were. You're just upset about finding a body. I understand."

"I doubt that you do, unless of course you tripped over a dead body and found yourself next to a blue guy in an ugly plaid suit."

Obviously the operator couldn't argue with her logic, because she didn't even try. Instead she said, "Ma'am, there should be an officer there. Can you see him?"

"I shut the front door, but even if I hadn't, I'm in the closet, so no, I can't see anyone."

She had to give the lady credit—not only did she treat calls about dead bodies with professional detachment, but the operator didn't even comment about the fact that Markie was now in the closet.

She just said, "Well, you can get out of the closet and open the door now. The officer's waiting on the porch."

"You're sure?" Markie asked, thinking of murderers in the bushes.

"Positive."

"Okay. Thanks."

She hung up the phone and climbed out of the closet. Her muscles felt overstretched, as if she'd been doing aerobics all day instead of squatting on the closet floor. She walked stiffly to the front door.

"Who's there?" she asked, just to be on the safe side.

"Police, ma'am."

She opened the door.

A tall, blond officer stood there. He had a baby face and didn't look nearly old enough to be a cop.

Heck, he barely looked old enough to shave.

It was hard to trust a cop whom you might have been babysitting only a few years back. Everything about him was shiny and crisp, as if he hadn't had a chance to break in his uniform yet.

Her day just kept getting worse. A baby officer had ridden to her rescue. The murderer would probably make mincemeat of him.

"Do you want to come in?" she asked, figuring she could lock both herself and her kiddie cop safely away in the house, away from the murderer.

"I'm Officer Manning. You called 911 about a body on the front porch?" he asked, ignoring her question.

Markie looked down and felt a spurt of relief. The officer might be young, but he was good at being a cop. He'd removed the body so that she didn't have to deal with it again.

He was considerate. His mother was probably so proud.

"Yes, I'm the one who called," Markie said. "Thanks for getting rid of it so quickly. I don't think I could stand looking at it again."

"I didn't get rid of it," the officer said. "When I arrived, there was no body here."

"There was a few minutes ago," she blurted out, staring at the spot under the officer's foot where the body had been.

The officer looked skeptical.

"I tell you, he was here. A dead man in a plaid suit, laid out in front of my door."

"You're sure he was dead? Maybe he was just a drunk who decided to sleep it off on your porch," the officer suggested.

It wasn't just what he said that set Markie's teeth on edge, but the look he gave her. A condescending, why-me-first-thing-on-a-Monday-morning sort of look.

"Listen, I know the difference between *dead* and *drunk*. This guy was *dead*."

"Yeah? How many dead guys have you seen before this?" he challenged.

That stopped her.

Other than her grandmother Ida, who had passed away two years ago, Markie had never even been to a funeral home before. "None really, at least not like this, but—"

"Markie?" came a voice she recognized immediately. A voice that came from a man she didn't want to see.

Zac Marshall. He gave a brief nod to the baby cop and then turned his attention back to her.

Detective Zac Marshall was as tall, dark and devilishly good-looking as ever. He had on black slacks, a black button-down shirt with a black tie, and, as a buffer against the current cold spell, a well-worn leather jacket.

Black leather, of course.

On some people all that black might have a somber, depressing effect.

On Zac, it just looked hot.

Not that Markie found him hot. She didn't want to find him anything at all.

It wouldn't be fair to say Zac was the last man on earth she wanted to see.

Joel Summers was the *last* man she wanted to see.

However, Zac Marshall was a close second-to-the-last-man.

"Zac," she said, trying to sound cool and disdainful, although starting her week with a disappearing corpse made anything but edgy and nervous a bit of a stretch.

"What happened?" Zac, the betrayer, asked.

Despite his clothes, there was nothing crisp and new about Zac. He'd been on the force long enough to look rather like his leather jacket, well-worn, broken in … and yummy.

Yummy?

Zac Marshall yummy?

Where had that come from?

Markie found many things yummy. Chocolate sundaes, chocolate cake, chocolate...well, anything chocolate. Ho Hos were very yummy. But not Zac.

Never Zac.

The stress of the day must have addled her hormones as well as her brain.

Or maybe all that black simply reminded her of chocolate, which was indeed yummy.

"She *claims* she found a body on the porch," Mr. Uniformly-Too-Young-To-Carry-A-Gun said with a hint of a sneer in his voice.

"*She* not only claims it," Markie said, "*she* did in fact find a body on her porch this morning. And *she* would appreciate it if you didn't refer to *her* as if *she* wasn't here."

Markie decided to ignore the kiddie cop and concentrate on Zac. And as long as she was ignoring things, she was going to ignore how totally yummy Zac looked. Better than chocolate even, darn it all.

"There *was* a dead body, Zac. I tripped over it, as a matter of fact. Look at the hole in my nylons." She held her leg up so both men could see.

"Okay, so you found a body. Any idea what could have happened to it?" Zac, not the officer, asked her.

If she hadn't decided to dislike Zac Marshall for the rest of this lifetime—and possibly a few more lifetimes after that—she might have felt more charitable toward him at that moment, because he had at least given her the benefit of a doubt. But he was number two on her least-liked list, and there wasn't much that would get someone off a Walkowicz list like that. Her family was known for holding grudges, and Markie had a killer grudge against Zac. One there was no recovering from.

"Markie? The body?" he prompted.

"I don't know what happened to it," she admitted. "I guess I lost it."

Lost it.

Markie's losing trend started when she was twelve and lost her younger brother, Danny, at the Smithsonian Air and Space Museum. Fifteen years later, she was pretty sure he still carried a grudge.

Not only did Danny still blame her for losing him, he swore he remembered the time she dropped him on his head when he was two. Markie doubted he really remembered that incident. She rather thought he'd simply heard the story so many times that he *thought* he remembered. But sometimes he would give her an odd sort of look, and she wondered.

Danny was the beginning of her losing streak.

Between then and now, she'd lost a lot of jobs and a number of fantasies. She'd lost a few pounds, but always seemed to gain those back. She'd lost her virginity to Stan Phillips.

Those were all small potatoes. Even Stan Phillips was small potatoes—in retrospect, Stan was especially small. Afterward, she wasn't sure losing her virginity to something that tiny actually counted.

But her biggest loss between the Danny incident and her missing corpse had happened last year when she lost a fiancé.

Losing a fiancé in and of itself, would have been a painfully big deal … an Idaho of a potato deal. But the fact that it happened on what would have been her wedding day made it even bigger.

The fact that it happened when Markie was dressed in Grandma Ida's gown, ready to walk down the aisle of St. Adalbert's Church, surrounded by family and friends, made it unbearably huge.

A freak county-fair-winning potato of a deal.

Someday she'd see that Joel Summers got his.

And if blaming Joel wasn't enough, she blamed Zac as well. She was sure that after Zac—her supposed very best childhood friend—failed to talk her out of marrying Joel, he'd tried talking Joel out of marrying her … and had succeeded with her louse of an ex-fiancé.

"Lost it?" Zac said, pulling her back from the small and freakishly large potatoes of her past to her missing-dead-body present. "How do you lose a corpse?"

"I don't know. It just wasn't here when the officer arrived."

Zac looked as if he were going to ask something else, so Markie said, "Let me start at the beginning. I got up late, probably because I stayed up to watch a Conan rerun last night, but I guess the fact I watched Conan isn't really important, unless you'd like me to recap his guests so I have an alibi."

"You don't even have a dead body, so I guess we can wait for that alibi."

Darn. Conan had on Ewan McGregor. She loved Conan. She loved Ewan McGregor, too. She would have enjoyed recapping the show.

Since her failed walk down the aisle, she hadn't dated much … hardly at all. Conan and his boy toy guests were her nightly dates. Thank goodness a cable network ran weekend Conan repeats, so she could watch him seven days a week if she wanted.

And she almost always wanted.

She'd be lost without her Conan.

But Zac didn't want to hear about her male companion of choice, so she forced her thoughts off her nightly pleasure and back to her Monday morning from hell.

"Fine," she said. "It was a repeat, but Conan's guest was Ewan McGregor, just in case you need to know."

She felt better for having mentioned both men.

"You were running late," Zac prompted.

"So I hurried, got dressed, which took longer because I have a meeting today and couldn't wear jeans. I didn't even stop for coffee. And I bought this new hazelnut blend I was dying to try this morning."

Dying to try… poor word choice there.

She gulped and continued without more prompting from Zac. "But I was late, so I threw open the front door, hurried out and tripped. Knocked the wind out of me. I turned around and there he was. Dead."

"You're sure?"

"Sure he was there or sure he was dead? Doesn't matter. Yes to both. He sort of looked blue and when I reached out to touch him, he was cold. Not just cold, but stiff. I guess that's why they call dead bodies stiffs on television shows."

That was a bit of insight she could have lived the rest of her natural existence without knowing.

"After you decided he was dead?"

"Well, I wasn't sure how he died and I got scared. I mean, what if he was murdered right here on my front porch? The railing and bushes sort of block the view from the street."

Her house was actually one of three connected houses in a row. Hers was on the left, then Mrs. Sullivan's, then Mrs. Galing's on the right. The steps came up the center of the porch, right in front of Mrs. Sullivan's door, but Markie's and Mrs. Galing's doors were sheltered by the railing and bushes that lined the small front yard.

She shivered at the thought of someone being murdered in front of her house. "Someone could have offed him here and no one would have known. And what if the killer was still around?"

She couldn't help but study the bushes, looking for some telltale sign the killer had been hiding there. "So, I got up, ran in the house, threw the dead bolt and chain in place and called 911. It took Dudley Do-Right there practically an eternity to get here. What if the murderer had tried to get me?"

"Did you look out the window to see if you could spot the murderer?"

"Are you kidding? I closed the drapes." She shook her head in disgust. "You know, men are weird. They think, *Murderer—confront him.* Women as a species are ever so much smarter. We think, *Murderer—hide.* That's what I did. I took the phone and hid in the closet, just in case whoever did the guy in was out there thinking about doing me in as well."

"Did you see anyone when you were outside?"

Markie thought a moment. "No."

"Anything unusual?"

"No, nothing. It was a normal, boring start to a normal, boring week."

"Other than that you found—"

"And lost," she interrupted.

"—and lost," he amended, "a dead body."

"Yes, that's about it. The officer arrived and I said something like, 'Oh, you already removed the body.' I was glad. I really didn't want to have to look it again. But he said, 'What body?' That's when I knew there was a problem."

"You couldn't figure out you had a problem when you found the dead body?" Zac asked with a certain Wiseguy tone to his voice and that slightly crooked grin that she knew so well.

Once upon a time, teasing her had been his primary source of entertainment.

She couldn't help but smile back. Just a small smile, because she didn't want him to think he was forgiven.

"Well, yeah, there was that," she admitted.

Markie had almost forgotten this facet of Zac. The funny, teasing side that could always make her feel better.

She'd almost forgotten it, but not quite.

She'd spent the last eleven months trying hard to will herself to not think about him. Unfortunately, she didn't have much willpower—the two boxes of Ho Hos in the cupboard proved that much—so she'd thought of him occasionally.

Without thinking, she still picked up the phone to call Zac every now and then, just as she'd done most of her life. To just share some little tidbit about her day with her best friend. She still wished he was around every time she watched a scary movie. After all, no matter what the monster was, it wouldn't dare mess with a supercop like Zac.

So, yes, she sort of missed him, not that she'd admit it. At least not to him.

Right now, she'd like nothing more than to throw herself into his arms and allow him to comfort her, but she stood her ground, feeling cold and alone. More cold and alone than she'd felt since the day Zac had convinced her fiancé to walk out on their wedding.

The thought of her wedding-that-wasn't gave her a small zing of anger, which warmed her a bit.

"So now what?" she asked.

"I guess we'll go take a look and see if we can find a body anywhere in the vicinity," Zac said.

"And if you can't?"

"I don't know what to tell you, Markie. We've never lost a dead body before."

"Neither have I," she said.

"But you see how it presents a problem?"

"Yeah. A problem."

Losing a dead body was worse than losing a fiancé.

If someone had asked her last week, Markie would have told them nothing could be as bad as walking down the aisle and finding only the priest waiting for you.

But that was last week.

This was this week.

And having lost a dead body, she could testify in court that it was definitely worse than losing Joel, who, it turned out, was no great loss at all.

2

Zac traipsed around the three connected homes, but didn't see any sign of a body. He wasn't sure what to make of Markie's missing corpse.

Once he heard her address on the radio followed by, "5292," he didn't know what to make of anything at all.

5292.

Markie's address and the code for a corpse.

At the moment Detective Zachary Marshall heard that combination on the radio, something twisted in his gut, something that still hadn't quite unwound. He was going to have nightmares for weeks.

It wouldn't be the first time Markie Walkowicz had given him nightmares. When she was ten, she'd decided to rescue a cat from the oak tree between their houses...a cat who wasn't interested in being rescued. When it clawed her, she'd lost her grip and fallen.

He'd been yelling at her to leave the cat alone when she slipped. Her fall seemed to last forever. There was nothing he could do but stand by helplessly and watch as she landed, breaking her leg.

When Markie had fallen from the tree, Zac had been able to run for help, to be there as she recovered. But Markie blamed him for Joel walking out on the wedding. She'd asked him if he'd talked to Joel after he'd talked to her that night and he'd said no. When she asked him why he'd tried to talk her out of the wedding then, he couldn't bring himself to admit the reason, to admit he was glad that Joel hadn't shown up.

No, he hadn't been responsible for Joel's leaving, but he'd felt a guilty sense of relief that there had been no wedding. That guilt helped keep him away from her. He wanted to give her some time and distance.

Days turned to weeks, weeks turned to months. Eleven to be exact.

He couldn't afford to think about Markie, about all the might-have-beens. He was a cop. He had a job to do. Now he had a missing corpse.

Not a normal investigation by any means.

But then, nothing about Markie had ever been what you'd call normal.

He walked the perimeter of her property, looking for any signs of the missing body, any signs that something out of the ordinary had happened here this morning.

He was worried about Markie and whatever was going on.

She looked as good as ever though. A little too thin. And maybe a bit tired. But good.

Her brown hair was longer than it used to be, and there was wariness in her dark eyes. Whatever happened today had scared her.

He wanted to take her in his arms and tell her it was all right.

God, how he'd missed her.

For the last eleven months, he'd tried to convince himself he didn't, but the long and the short of it was he did. But she hadn't missed him at all. There had been no welcoming smile on her face, no tears and *glad-you're-here*.

She still blamed him ... he could see it in her expression.

And maybe she was right in blaming him, but not for the reasons she'd give if asked. She was right because he'd known all along that Joel Summers wasn't the man for her.

A year ago Zac might have said that *he* was the man for her—that's what he'd tried to tell her the night before her wedding, but he'd never gotten to the I-love-you part. When she heard "Don't marry Joel tomorrow" she began to profess her undying love for her fiancé. After that, confessing his own feelings seemed pointless.

Thankfully, he was over the remnants of his childhood crush.

At least, most of the time he was over it. Eleven months of separation had seen to that. But that call today convinced him there still might be a bit of it lingering deep within his psyche. But he could ignore those small pieces of his, well, infatuation.

What he couldn't ignore was that he missed Markie's friendship.

He missed laughing with her.

He missed fighting with her.

He just missed her. Period.

But once a Walkowicz held a grudge against someone, they didn't let go.

Markie still held one against Sylvia Carson, who, back in ninth grade, had commented on how big Markie's feet had looked.

Someone who could carry a grudge for something like that for so long—well, Zac knew the odds of getting back in Markie's good graces were slim to nil.

All he could do was his job.

There was no sign of a corpse in the immediate area. Time to knock on doors and question neighbors.

He needed answers for Markie's sake. It was clear that Manning thought she was nuts.

Zac knew she *was* nuts, but not the kind of crazy that made up dead bodies on the porch.

He knocked on her middle neighbor's door and flashed his badge when someone hollered, "Who is it?"

"Detective Zac Marshall. I'm with the Philadelphia Police Department, ma'am."

The door opened slowly. A hefty, gray-haired lady, probably in her late sixties or early seventies, looked at him worriedly. "Yes?"

"You might have noticed the commotion next door." He jerked his head towards Markie's.

"No, no. I was just sitting in my chair watching television. My morning show's on. I never miss it. Never move from my chair until it's over. So, I didn't notice anything."

"Your neighbor, Markie Walkowicz, found a man outside her front door this morning."

Zac purposely didn't mention that Markie thought the man in question was dead. No need to make the rather nervous-looking lady more nervous.

"I wondered if you saw or heard something, anything unusual?"

"I don't know anything about a man. I'm a widow and I mind my own business."

"You're sure you didn't see anything? You can tell me." He dropped his voice to a conspiratorial whisper. "I won't tell anyone else."

For a moment the woman hesitated, but then she shook her head. "Young man, I said I didn't see anybody. I can hardly see at all, even with my glasses on. Cataract on my right eye. I go in for surgery next month. So I'm of no help to you."

"Well, thank you for your time. I'll go question the neighbor on the other side."

"It's Monday. Gladys is at the beauty salon this morning. Gladys is always at the beauty salon Monday mornings. She likes to start her week with her hair done."

"Okay. I'll try across the street. Well, thank you, ma'am."

He paused and said, "Oh, by the way, could I have your name for my report?"

"Sullivan. Mrs. Beatrice Sullivan."

"Well, thank you, Mrs. Sullivan. If you happen to think of anything else, here's my card. Call me."

She took the card, gave him a quick nod and then shut the door in his face.

Zac didn't know what to make of it. He knocked on the other neighbors' doors, but no one seemed to be around. He'd have to come back later and try.

He went back to Markie's.

"Did you find anything?" she asked, ushering him out of the foyer and into the living room, which just showed how rattled she was. If it wasn't for the corpse, he knew she would never have let him into her home.

Zac studied her living room.

Markie had inherited the house from her grandmother two years ago. Tenants had rented it the first year, but after Joel left her at the altar, she'd moved from her Center City apartment into the house.

Even if Markie wasn't speaking to Zac, keeping track of her wasn't hard. His mother and hers were best friends, as well as neighbors. So he'd heard when she moved back into the Port Richmond neighborhood.

The room was bigger than the living room at her apartment, but despite the additional space, it was packed. She'd bought new shelves, which lined one entire wall. Books were shelved helter-skelter. A big sofa and a huge, overstuffed chair with mismatched fabrics sat invitingly in front of a huge fireplace. An entertainment center rounded out the furniture.

The room was full, sort of cluttered, but cozy. It suited Markie.

"Did you find anything?" she asked again.

He shook his head. "I don't know what to make of it, what to say."

"Say you found the body," she said, sounding unsure and nervous.

"I didn't. The neighborhood is pretty deserted this time of day. I just found your neighbor, Mrs. Sullivan, at home and she didn't hear or see anything."

"So now what?"

"Well, we'll canvass the other neighbors, but unless something else turns up, I'm afraid the investigation is over."

"Over? There may be a crazed murderer roaming our neighborhood, and you're just going to let him continue to maim and terrorize?"

"We have no evidence anyone was maimed or terrorized. As a matter of fact, we have no evidence that a crime was committed. There is no body."

"I know there is. I saw it. I tripped over it. And as for maimed and terrorized, I was both. Not that you care. Not that you ever cared."

He knew they were no longer talking about corpses, but were now talking about Joel. "Markie, that's not fair."

"Not fair is having a beautiful wedding, with no groom because your supposed friend talked him out of marrying you."

"I know that's what you said in the heat of the moment, right after the wedding—"

"There was no wedding, remember?"

"The almost-wedding," he corrected himself. "But do you really think I tried to talk him out of marrying you?"

"You tried to talk me out of marrying him."

It was time to tell the truth … the whole truth and nothing but the truth. She'd had eleven months to heal.

"Listen, Markie—" He stopped short when his radio squawked.

He put the mike to his mouth. "Marshall."

"Riker wants to see you in his office ASAP," the operator said.

"Be there in five." He turned to Markie. "This isn't finished."

"You'll be back to investigate my missing body?"

"There's nothing to investigate. No body, no crime."

"Fine." She walked to the front door and opened it, holding it, waiting for him to leave.

"But Markie, I'll be back to finish our discussion on just what I did and did not do at or before your wedding."

"My almost-wedding. But don't bother coming to discuss it. There's nothing you can say." Her voice was flat, devoid of emotion.

He walked up to the door and stopped right in front of her. "It's been almost a year. I think it's more than time to discuss things."

He hurried toward his car before Markie could find a retort.

She liked to have the last word. But this time, he'd managed it. He felt rather smug as he opened the car door.

"Discuss things without me," Markie yelled. "If you're not investigating the dead body, then we have nothing to say."

She slammed her front door.

Yeah, Markie liked having the last word, but that wasn't the last of it.

Not by a long shot.

3

"**O**n the Mark. If we can't do the job, we know who can. How may I help you?"

Markie nervously glanced at the glass door for about the thousandth time.

She'd been jumpy all day.

That's what finding a corpse in the morning did to a person. Although she supposed finding a corpse in the afternoon or evening would have pretty much the same effect.

Concentrate on work, she reminded herself not for the first time since she got into the office.

Thankfully, she'd made it to her appointment at the bank and then arrived at the office, where she'd had a bunch of calls waiting for her.

Normally, she was in the office most mornings and went out into the field in the afternoon, but today was not normal... not by a long shot. Being boss of a one-woman company meant she could juggle things as she wanted them.

Returning calls, rescheduling jobs—it kept her busy all afternoon. Thankfully, she had a few small jobs to do before she went home—she wasn't sure she could face her porch.

"Hello, Markie. It's Mr. Nauss," said the voice on the other end of the phone line. "My gutter is leaking every time the sun shines, which I know is rare in the winter in Philly. But when we do get a hint of brightness, the ice melts just enough for the thing to leak. The huge icicles are a hazard. Any chance you could come over and fix it?"

She consulted her planner. She was booked, but she'd figure something out for Mr. Nauss.

"I'll stop by tomorrow and take a look," she promised. "But it will have to be early. Say about seven, on my way into work?"

Mr. Nauss was an early riser, she knew from past experience. And his home wasn't far from hers.

"Sounds good," he said.

Looking at gutters was a lot easier than looking for dead bodies. After the police had left, she'd gone around her northeastern Philadelphia neighborhood herself, sure that Zac had missed something, probably just to spite her. But there was nothing.

Nada.

She'd talked to Mrs. Sullivan, but her neighbor hadn't seen or heard anything, and there was no one else around to question.

No. No more thinking about this morning. She was thinking about gutters.

"Great," she said to Mr. Nauss. "I'll see you then."

"You're a godsend, Markie. A real sweetie."

"I bet you say that to all the girls."

"Yes, but with you I mean it," he joked. "I'll see you in the morning."

Markie was smiling as she hung up the phone, her troubles momentarily forgotten.

Mr. Nauss was one of her favorite clients. He was why she'd started On the Mark. Allowing Mr. Nauss and others like him—people who just needed a little help in order to remain in their homes and be independent—that was something worthwhile.

It was as if all those years of wandering, looking for her niche, working a multitude of jobs, all of it had been so she could do this…run On the Mark.

She'd worked construction, painted, waited tables, washed dishes, done lawn maintenance…the list was long and varied. But all of those jobs had given her the experience she needed to run On the Mark.

Like her slogan said, if she couldn't do a job, then she knew who could. She had contacts in almost every service industry there was in Philadelphia.

In the past ten months, her small business had grown faster than she'd ever imagined it could. Originally, she'd run it out of her house; then, about six months ago she'd lucked into this office space. It was really not much more than a glorified room with big windows, but the rent in the Port Richmond neighborhood had been affordable, more affordable than something in Center City. It was close to home. But most importantly, it was hers.

Having an office seemed to make her business more *real*.

Things went from good to better, and now she was even thinking about taking on an employee. Maybe this spring, when people's thoughts turned to sprucing up the house. She'd hire someone to take care of the office work. It would free her up to be out and about. That's what she liked best. She'd—

The small bell on the front door of her store jangled.

Markie jumped at the sound. Her nerves were still rather hair-trigger.

Her mother walked in. A sense of relief flooded through her system—no would-be murderer here. But quick on its heels came a feeling of apprehension.

Her mother was wearing one of *those looks.*

Estelle Walkowicz was on a mission and Markie realized she was the mission's target.

Her mother marched up to the desk and stopped. Back straight, arms crossed over her ample chest, her hazel eyes boring into Markie's. "What did you do now?"

"Pardon?"

I begged you to go to college, to be a teacher," her mother said, starting right in with a familiar lament. "Teachers are highly respected women—"

Markie interrupted. "And men."

Her mother ignored her. "—women who spend their lives giving to the community, educating the next generation. Selfless. Honorable. Teachers get married and give their mothers grandchildren. Teachers do not go around telling other people stories about dead bodies on their front porches."

"I bet teachers would tell stories about dead bodies if they found a corpse on the porch." Markie paused. "Don't you want to ask how I am, Mom? What if whoever did in that poor man had tried to kill me as well? Aren't you the least bit concerned?"

"There was no body. At least, that's what Paula said."

Paula.

Paula Marshall. Her mother's best friend and next-door neighbor for the last thirty years.

Paula Marshall—Detective Zachary Marshall's mother.

Zac had run tattling to his mother?

He'd stabbed her in the back again?

Any redemption he'd earned with today's encounter disappeared in a flash.

"Mrs. Marshall's wrong. There was a body on my porch. It disappeared while I was calling 911."

Her mother didn't say anything, just continued giving Markie the eye.

"Mom, there *was* a body. I don't know what happened to it."

"If you'd been a teacher—"

"There still would have been a body on my porch this morning."

"Ah," her mother said, uncrossing her arms long enough to give Markie one good finger waggle and then crossing them again. "Ah, but if you'd been a teacher, you'd be married and have children, so there would have been witnesses, other people to back up your crazy story."

"Would you really want your grandchildren exposed to a corpse?"

That stopped her mother.

"You're right. But that's it. No more dead bodies. It's all over the neighborhood. And worrying about you is making my hair turn gray."

To the best of her knowledge, Markie had been making her mother's hair turn gray since the day she was born. Not that anyone would know. Her mother's hair was always changing colors, but of all the colors it had been, gray was never one of them.

Today, it was a lovely shade of auburn.

"Thank goodness for Bella," Markie said. "No one would ever know there was a gray hair on your head because she does a great dye job."

"You're testing even her skills," her mother grumbled.

"I'll do my best to avoid corpses in the future, Mom." That was a promise she could wholeheartedly make.

No more corpses before coffee for Marquette Ann Walkowicz.

None after coffee either, for that matter.

"'And speaking of hair," her mother said, "why don't you do something with yours? Bella would love to do it for you. You know how busy she is at the salon, but I have connections. I can get you in."

"Thanks, but I don't have time right now. I got a late start today. I don't suppose you'd like to spend some time in the office? Any day this week would be a help."

Her mother gave a large, put-upon sigh. "I suppose I could stand getting out a couple days."

Her mother often filled in at the office when Markie needed help.

"Tomorrow at eight?"

"I'll be here." With that, Estelle Walkowicz started toward the door. Then she turned and said, "I was worried and needed to see for myself you were all right," and hurried out before Markie could say anything in response.

Estelle Walkowicz didn't like overt displays of emotion, but Markie knew her mother loved her.

Markie sighed.

And she loved her mother.

Honestly and truly.

"And when you're done, I'll get you a bowl of my *pasta e fagiole*," Mrs. Carrera chirped from her seat at the kitchen table.

Markie's stomach growled. She'd worked right through lunch.

As soon as she fixed Mrs. Carrera's leaky sink, her workday was over.

Of course, it was almost seven in the evening and if today had been a normal day, she would have been finished hours ago.

"It's lucky for you that I made a pot today. You're all skin and bones and my *pasta e fagiole* is just the thing to fatten you up. A man likes a bit of padding, my mother always said."

Markie laughed. "That would be great, Mrs. Carrera."

She always tried to schedule jobs for Mrs. Carrera late in the day because nothing gave the older lady more delight than feeding people…Markie in particular. And it truly was Markie's pleasure to oblige.

"I'll be right back, dear," Mrs. Carrera said.

"No problem." Markie's mind was on the soup…thinking about it made her mouth water as she wrestled with the obstinate bolt. The darned thing just wasn't cooperating.

Markie swore quietly.

"Tut, tut, tut. That's no way for a lady to talk."

Zac.

Markie sat straight up…under the sink.

And since the sink was set at a rather average height, a height that was definitely shorter than Markie was in a sitting position, she conked her head smartly against it.

"Zac," she said, turning his name into a curse word. She wiggled out from under the sink, rubbing her head. "What do you want?"

"Come on, Markie. I know you're glad to see me, but don't gush so much. It's embarrassing," he teased, taking the seat Mrs. Carrera had vacated.

Markie wasn't in the mood for Zac Marshall's odd sense of humor. This had to go down as the worst Monday in the history of the world and, as she rubbed the goose egg that was growing at alarming speed, it didn't appear to be getting any better.

"How did you find me?"

"Come on, Markie, I'm a detective. Give me some credit."

"I'm not giving you anything. You told your mother about the body on my porch," she accused.

"I did not. I left your house and was pretty much tied up at the office ever since. I haven't spoken to my mother all day."

"Well, your mother told my mother."

"Oh, no. Estelle called?" he asked, all sympathetic. Having grown up next door to Markie, he couldn't help but be well aware of her mother's more *interesting* personality traits.

"Worse. She came by. Did you know that school teachers never find bodies on their porches?"

He smiled. "I imagine they don't."

"They also marry and have children who can witness said corpses if one were to have them on one's porch."

He chuckled and said, "Sorry."

"Me, too," Markie said. "So if you didn't rat me out to your mother, how did she know?"

"Manning, maybe," Zac said. "That first officer at your house today."

"That baby cop called your mom?"

"No. Worse. Matt Manning's Bella-at-the-hair-salon's nephew."

Bella? Otherwise known as the town crier? The baby cop was her nephew?

"Oh, no." This just went to prove the old saying that things could always get worse…much worse. "If Bella knows, then everyone knows."

This was truly the Monday from hell, a never-ending, eternal sort of hell.

Feeling bone-tired, Markie said, "What do you want, Zac?"

"Dinner," he said.

"Pardon?"

"I want you to come out to dinner with me," he said slowly and succinctly.

"Dinner?" She shook her head. "I don't think that would be wise. We can't go back. Things have changed. We've both moved on."

"I'm not talking about going back." He frowned, which made his brow wrinkle.

Once upon a time, Markie would have tried to tease him out of the expression, but now she was the cause of it and would leave it alone.

"I know things have changed," he said. "I'm talking about dinner so we can talk about the case."

"You said there was no case without a body, and it seems I've lost the body, so excuse me if I don't see why we would need to have dinner."

"Maybe we'll be able to come up with a few ideas about what could have happened to the body."

"I've spent the day thinking about it, without coming up with a single idea. I can't imagine that dinner will help me think of anything."

She realized he wasn't listening, but was studying her tool chest by the sink.

She looked but didn't see anything out of the ordinary. "What?"

"This," he said. "It's great."

"My tool chest is great?"

"No, On the Mark. I've been making calls... seems business is good."

"The office isn't much, but it's a step up from running things in the house, and it's mine. But it's the clients, really. I've almost got enough steady business to hire someone, not just rely on my mother filling in there when I get swamped."

"You've been busy."

"It's not like I had anything else to do with my time. Someone chased away my fiancé."

"Markie—"

She held up her hand. "Forget I mentioned that. Like I said, there's no going back, and that should mean we don't fall back on pointless recriminations. I don't want to talk about Joel."

"How about talking about your business?" he asked. "I'd like to hear more."

Dinner.

The offer was tempting.

Markie really didn't want to go home, didn't want to be alone. She most certainly didn't want to see her front porch.

And talking about On the Mark was always a pleasure.

But dinner with Zac? The man who was number two on her least-liked list.

Well, Zac was better than a corpse. Maybe that made him number three. Joel, corpses, then Zac.

Or maybe, corpses, Joel, then Zac.

No, definitely Joel, corpses, then Zac.

No matter how you sliced it, Zac was now third, not second on her least-liked list.

"Mrs. Carrera was kind enough to offer me *pasta e fagiole,* I can't say no now … but talking about the business … it's something I never get tired of," she said slowly, not exactly accepting.

"So, what if you ask for a rain check on the soup, we get dinner instead and talk about your business and your missing body?"

The frown and furrowed brow were gone. In their place was that endearing smile again. Zac had spent a lifetime perfecting that particular expression.

"You know that look doesn't work on me," she pointed out.

"Ah, but I also know what will … Captain Nemo's."

"Zac, that's not fair."

Captain Nemo's was a restaurant known for its artery-clogging dinners. Fried shrimp. Fried fish. Fried...fried anything. It was ambrosia, and just what her stress-strained body needed to coat and soothe her frazzled nerves.

"And to make it even more irresistible," he said, "I called ahead and told them it was your birthday."

Birthdays at Captain Nemo's.

Markie had celebrated at least thirty-five birthdays there. And the fact that she was only twenty-seven might make that seem impossible, but she was as addicted to their birthday cake as she was to their fish and chips. She had a *birthday* as often as she thought she could get away with it.

"Fine," she said, trying to maintain an air of disinterest, even though the mere mention of the Captain's was enough to spur a lot of interest. "I'll see if Mrs. Carrera will let me have the *pasta e fagiole* to go and have dinner with you, but only to discuss dead bodies and talk about the business. You can even talk about how the detective stuff is going, but since you didn't detect my missing corpse, that might be a short discussion."

"Now, that has to go down in the history books as the most original dinner acceptance ever," he said with a wry tone. "And for the record, I did manage to find you."

"I'm not out for an award, just answers."

"Answers and Captain Nemo's birthday cake," he said, grinning again.

Markie couldn't help a small smile of her own. "Yeah, the Captain ranks right up there with the answer part."

Dinner with Zac.

Despite the fact it was at her favorite restaurant, she shouldn't be smiling. As a matter of fact, she shouldn't be going at all.

But the small fizzy feeling in the pit of her stomach didn't feel like apprehension … no, it felt like anticipation.

Yesterday, she'd almost forgotten about Zac Marshall and she certainly wouldn't have believed she'd be anticipating dinner with him today.

Look how much difference twenty-four hours could make.

"So," she said as she sat at the table at Captain Nemo's an hour later.

It was her favorite table. The one under the giant shark.

Of course, as she and Zac sat there languishing in awkward silence she was envisioning the shark jumping off the wall and chomping on him.

It was a big shark.

She bet it could manage to swallow Zac in just a couple bites.

Three at the most.

"What's that smile for?" he asked.

"Just thinking," she said.

Yeah, Jaws could definitely finish off Zac in no more than three bites.

Zac's eyes narrowed as he studied her. "It's dangerous when a Walkowicz thinks too much."

"Sometimes it is. Remember Joey Witkowski?"

Zac groaned. "It took two weeks for him to stop jumping back every time he opened his locker."

He paused a moment and added softly, "And it's taken us eleven months to be ready to talk about Joel—"

"No. We're not ready. I'm not ready."

Rather than think about her once-upon-a-time-fiancé, she scanned the room for the waiter. Maybe she should have gotten a salad, but salads seemed too healthy a food to be eaten at the Captain's. She didn't come here for vitamins. She came for grease.

Over the last year her eating habits had become...well, less habitual.

Between the business growing and keeping up with her crazy family, she frequently forgot to eat.

Some days, she got by on just coffee and...well, coffee. She just hadn't had much of an appetite, but tonight, despite the less-than-perfect company, she was starving.

Yes, even though a salad was healthy, it probably wouldn't have taken care of the pangs of hunger.

"So what do you want to talk about?" Zac finally said.

"Dead bodies?"

He shook his head. "Nothing to report."

Zac still had that weird piece of hair on his left side. No matter what he did, it sort of fell over his eye. She used to brush it back all the time. She fought back the urge to do so now. She was sure she'd lost that right.

"Do you think I imagined it?"

"No."

They lapsed into another silence.

Finally Zac said, "So, you opened your own business."

"Yes." She knew he was trying to strike up a conversation, but she wasn't sure she remembered how to converse with him. Last year at this time, she'd have bubbled over telling him all about her plans for On the Mark, but now?

She just didn't see the point. He hadn't found her dead body, so after tonight there was no reason to see him again, no reason to get all chummy.

"That was an opportunity for you to tell me more about it," he scolded.

She shrugged. "I told you most of it this afternoon. My mother says I'm a glorified handyman."

Where was that waiter?

"Woman."

"Pardon?" she asked.

"You're a handywoman. No one would ever mistake you for a man, handy or otherwise." He shot her a grin.

"Thanks, I think."

"You're welcome."

The waiter came and brought their food. Huge plates of mouth-watering fish and chips.

Salvation.

Markie was glad to have something legitimate to do.

She bit into her fish.

Mmm.

"I forgot how much I love the Captain's," she said as that first bite slid its well-greased way down her throat.

"You haven't come here much?"

"No. It wasn't the same ..." *without you* is what she almost said, but she changed it in time and said, "after everything that happened."

"Do you remember the last time you celebrated a birthday here?" he asked.

She couldn't help but smile at the memory. "And it was the same waiter who'd waited on my last *birthday*."

"And he said, 'Didn't you just have a birthday last month?'"

She wanted to remain aloof, but the memory was too sweet. She was caught up in it and chuckled. "And I said, 'No, that was my twin sister.'"

Zac chuckled along with her. "That was bad enough, but then you went into that lengthy explanation—"

"About how my mother was pregnant and gave birth to my sister prematurely, but the doctors gave her drugs so she could carry me another month to term. And that's why my identical twin didn't have the same birthday."

This is what she'd missed, Markie realized suddenly. She'd shared so much with Zac.

Not only shared laughter. A history.

Zac was two years older. He'd even been the one to teach her how to ride a two-wheeler. Of course, his idea of teaching had been to take her to the top of a hill, plop her on the bike and then push.

It was sort of the sink-or-swim philosophy. Come to think of it, that's how he'd taught her to swim as well—a quick push off the edge of the pool.

"You're doing it again," he said.

"What?"

"Smiling." His voice softened and he asked, "What were you thinking about this time?"

"That I've missed this. No one other than my family knows me like you do. Actually, not even my family knows me like you do." Saying that out loud stopped her short. "Yeah, like they don't know about Stan Phillips and how you convinced him that when I said it was over, it was—even if he didn't want it to be."

"He wasn't the sharpest tool in the chest, but he did finally get it after I helped him understand it."

Markie was pretty sure that Zac's explanation had been a bit more than just verbal. Stan had come to school the next day with a black eye.

Zac had always been her defender, her confidant, her friend. That's why she'd been so hurt over the whole Joel thing. "Anyway, that's what I was thinking. About how I missed having someone who knew me like that."

"I've been here," he reminded her.

"I know. But I wasn't ready."

"And now?"

Did she want to let Zac back into her life?

"Maybe," she said.

She took a bite of her fish. The taste was total ambrosia. She sighed. "It's as good as I remember."

Zac wasn't sure if Markie was talking about sharing a meal with him, or the fish. But whichever was as good as she remembered, her smile was doing something to him.

He watched her enjoy her dinner. She'd take a bite and then give a little sigh of contentment.

Those sighs did things to him, things they shouldn't.

They always had.

Not that Markie ever noticed. She saw him as a child-hood friend, a buddy, a neighbor. Nothing more.

Eventually, he'd learned to settle for just her friendship, but that didn't stop her from affecting him. Some times worse than others.

Watching her savor her meal was one of those times.

He speared a bite of his fish.

At least the evening seemed to be going well. Maybe they could reestablish their friendship.

Maybe—

"Is that my Markie?" someone said, interrupting Zac's thoughts.

He looked up and groaned.

"The Port Richmond brigade," he quickly whispered to Markie, who immediately groaned.

Markie's mother, his mother, his twin aunts, Erin and Andrea, plus Bella Wodarski descended on their table.

"Well, now, isn't this interesting," Markie's mom practically cooed.

Cooing women gave Zac hives.

His mom smiled and patted his head as if he were nine. "I always told you," she said to Estelle Walkowicz, "that what your Markie needed was a good man like my Zac."

His twin aunts bobbed their heads and said in unison, "Yes, you always told us, too."

"I remember the two of you playing doctor when you were … what was it, Paula?" Markie's mom said.

"Oh, maybe four and six," his mother answered. "Anyway, Markie, dear, you have Zac bring you to dinner."

"And Zac, you know you're welcome at our house any time," Markie's mother, not to be outdone, offered.

"I hate to be a party pooper," Bella Wodarski said, "but isn't anyone the least bit concerned that Zac is dating … well, far be it from me to cast stones, but Markie, honey, before you and Zac get all permanent, maybe you should see a doctor about your hallucinations."

"My daughter does not have hallucinations," Markie's mother said.

"Well, my nephew Matt said she didn't have a dead body on her porch," Bella argued. "So either it walked off, or wasn't there to begin with."

"Maybe someone took it," Markie's mom said.

Zac liked that Mrs. Walkowicz was sticking up for Markie.

He glanced over at Markie. Her face had turned pink with embarrassment.

"It was nice to see you ladies," he said in a bid to get them to leave.

"Who would take a dead body?" Bella asked, ignoring his attempt. "None of the neighbors saw it. The cops didn't see it. Just poor, nutty Markie."

She turned to Markie and said, "Go to the doctor, dear, before it's too late. They have medication for just about everything these days."

"And you probably know, Bella, because you've been on medication for years," Markie's mom said.

"Please," Markie said. "No fighting. I don't know what happened to the body, but Bella, no matter what your nephew said, I didn't imagine it. I tripped over it."

"See," Markie's mom said.

"Maybe that's it," his aunt Erin said. "Maybe Markie tripped coming out of her house and hit her head."

"That would explain why she thinks she saw a dead body. It was a concussion," Aunt Andrea finished. "You know our great uncle Dworavitch hit his head once and couldn't spell his own name for a week."

Erin said, "He never spelled Dworavitch right, even without a knock on the noggin."

"Concussions don't make you see bodies. Insanity does," Bella said.

"Bella," all four women said in unison.

"Listen, I've got to go," Markie announced.

She stood and hurried toward the door.

"Excuse me," Zac said, ready to run after her, but Bella was in front of him and grabbed his shoulder.

"Far be it from me to get in the middle of things, but my nephew seems to think Markie is nuttier than a bowl of pecans. Now, it's understandable, considering the way her fiancé dumped her last year, but since your mother and her mother won't say it, I will. Be careful, Zac. Crazy women don't make good girlfriends."

Bella stepped aside and Zac bolted for the door. He opened it, but all he saw was an empty street.

"Sir," the waitress said, chasing after him. "You forgot to pay your bill."

He sighed and walked back into Captain Nemo's.

Things had been going so well, all things considered. And now, Markie was gone … and she hadn't even waited for her birthday cake.

4

After spending a restless night tossing and turning, Markie arrived at On the Mark much earlier than she'd expected to the next morning. Dreams of plaid-suited bodies had traded off with dreams of Zac all night. Finally around five o'clock, she gave up trying to sleep.

She couldn't decide which of her dreams was more disturbing.

She'd yawned her way through fixing Mr. Nauss's gutters and now all she needed was a few moments of quiet and a big cup of caffeine.

The bell chimed merrily as she walked into the office. She could almost taste the hazelnut blend, feel the peace of walking into her own business—a business she'd built single-handedly.

It was just what she needed.

She stopped. Her mother was sitting at the desk, an expression on her face that told Markie there would be no peace here. If she was lucky she might get some coffee though.

"Morning, Mom," she said as she headed toward the table in the back.

Her mother got up from the desk and followed her. "So, what's going on between you and Zac?"

Ah, her mother had started the coffee, which meant not only was she going to get a cup, it would be a *good* cup at that.

Markie poured a mug and took a sip before answering. "Me and Zac? Would you believe me if I said absolutely nothing?"

"No," her mother replied.

Markie took another sip and sighed. "I didn't figure you would, but it's the truth. The only thing going on with Zac and I is one missing dead body."

"Don't start with that story about a body again. There was no body."

"I can't start again because I never stopped with the story about the body, and yes there was."

"Everyone says you're nuts," her mother tried. "Bella's been telling your disappearing corpse story to everyone who walks into the salon. Do you want people talking about you?"

"Someone once told me that I should ignore what people say."

"Well, that someone was a fool," her mother said with a decisive humph.

"That someone was you," Markie said, feeling triumphant.

Ha.

She'd scored a point on her mom. That rarely happened.

"Zac was here when I got here. He left you that." She pointed to a small white box on the counter.

Markie thought she recognized the type of container and opened it slowly, almost reverently.

Ahh.

She was right, it was a take-out box from Captain Nemo's. Zac had brought her small single-serving birthday cake from last night.

She'd kicked herself for forgetting about it.

There was even a plastic fork in the box.

She took a bite, then chased it down with a sip of coffee. It might not be the breakfast of champions, but it was just what she needed.

"You had another birthday?" her mother said with a tsk.

Markie had another bite in her mouth, so she simply nodded.

Maybe her mother would let the body conversation die.

Oh, that didn't sound right, even in her head.

She took another bite.

"Your brother called yesterday," her mother said.

Ah, talking about Danny. That was better.

"Even he has heard about your body," her mom said.

Rats.

"He said that after the way you lost him in Washington that time, it's no surprise to him that you could lose a corpse."

Markie made a mental note to get Danny back for that one. "Do you think he's ever going to forgive me?"

"No." Her mother paused. "And he's not going to forgive you for the time you dropped him on his head either. But, speaking of Danny, I have a question to ask you."

"Shoot." She took another bite of cake.

"Is your brother gay?" her mother asked.

Markie choked on the cake and tried to clear her throat by taking a gulp of coffee … coffee that was still hot.

Her tongue was scalded, but at least she could breathe.

Markie had expected her mother to ask if maybe they could plan a big family meal. Her mom liked to get them all together every month or so.

But Danny gay?

She didn't know what to say other than, "No."

"Are you sure? I mean, would you tell me if he was?"

"Yes, I would tell you, and yes, I'm as sure as a sister can be."

Her mom sighed. "It's not that I wouldn't love him if he was gay. Heaven knows my uncle Leo was pretty flaming. I mean, he was out of the closet before most people acknowledged there was a closet. We all loved him to death. As a matter of fact, I took Leo with me to buy my prom dress my senior year. It might sound like a stereotype, but the man had a keen sense of fashion. So, I could handle Danny's being gay. I just couldn't handle him thinking he had to hide it from me."

Markie gave her mother a quick hug. "Well, I think you can stop worrying. I don't think Danny's gay."

"So why isn't he dating? Not in months."

"I haven't dated in months, but that doesn't mean I'm gay."

"No," her mother agreed, "but you have a reason. That creep Joel. And you have dated. Last night. Dinner with Zac."

How did her mom do it?

Every time Markie thought she'd moved from an uncomfortable topic, her mother was able to circle the conversation back around to it so effortlessly.

"It wasn't a date. It was a…a business meeting. And speaking of business, I have a bunch of appointments today."

"But—"

"Sorry, Mom." She took the last bite of cake, gulped down the remainder of her coffee and headed for the door. "Gotta run."

"But—"

"Oh, if you have time, maybe you could draft a job description? I think in the next month or so I'm going to start looking for an employee."

"Markie, about you and Zac…"

"There's nothing to tell. It was business. Listen, I'm sorry, Mom. Like I said, gotta run. Lots of work today. That's why I asked you to come in. I'll check in with you later."

Markie didn't know a lot of things, but she was certain that there was absolutely nothing at all going on between her and Zac Marshall.

Though it had been nice of him to rescue her cake and drop it off this morning.

She hurried out to her car and wished she'd brought another cup of coffee with her.

She glanced at her watch. She had a half hour until her next appointment. She could just stop somewhere and grab a cup, or she could head to her friend and former roommate, Babs's.

It was a no-brainer.

She'd head to Babs's and let her friend assure her that just because dead bodies were disappearing from her front porch, that didn't mean she was crazy.

Did it?

Markie pulled up in front of her old Center City apartment. Babs still lived there.

Babs was actually Betty Ann Kreszewski.

Her friend hated the name.

Babs wasn't sure she liked *Babs* either, but back in grade school she'd decided her neighborhood nickname was much better than Betty Ann, which is what the nuns at St. Adalbert's insisted on calling her for the entire nine years—kindergarten through eighth grade—they'd spent there.

Markie had always thought being called Betty Ann was decidedly better than being called Marquette.

Over the years, they'd had many heated arguments about whose name was worse. They'd also frequently theorized about what their respective mothers had been smoking when they'd come up with their names.

Markie felt better walking toward her old Broad Street apartment. She didn't miss living in Center City, the heart of Philly—her Port Richmond neighborhood was more her style. But she did miss seeing Babs every day.

Seeing her was just what Markie needed.

Although once Babs found out she'd had dinner with Zac, she might conclude a bit of sanity impairment existed. And it was a given that Babs would find out. There was no keeping secrets from Babs.

And vice versa.

Babs had insisted she keep a key, so Markie let herself in and hiked up the three flights of stairs to the apartment.

As she made the trek, she figured Babs had better offer a donut or a bagel with the coffee, because climbing up to the apartment was a workout and her Captain Nemo's cake wasn't going to be enough to sustain her.

One of the advantages to moving to Grandma Ida's old house was a lot fewer stairs.

Markie tapped on the apartment door, then simply unlocked it. "Hey, sleepyhead."

She walked to the kitchen to start the coffee.

When Markie began planning to move out after she was married, Babs made the move to work at home. She quit her job at a firm and began to work as a freelance graphic designer.

So far, she was doing all right. And the great thing was, Markie could almost always count on finding her there.

Babs rarely went out, since her ex—known with absolutely no affection at all as *the weenie*—had broken up with her.

Markie and Babs had not only shared a friendship and an apartment, but they shared horrible taste in men.

Markie made the coffee and thought, not for the first time, that it was time to get Babs out in the dating game again.

To the best of her knowledge, other than business meetings, the last time Babs had gone out was to a Walkowicz family dinner. Not much of a date there.

"Hey, Babs, are you ever getting out of bed, you slug?" she called again.

Yeah, taking Babs out on the town for an evening of wine and men. That was just the thing to get missing corpses and Zac Marshall off her mind.

Babs quietly opened her bedroom door, then shut it. "Shh."

"What?" Markie asked at the same moment she spotted a pair of men's boots on the living room floor and she knew. "You've got a man in there, don't you?"

"Yes," Babs said, sinking onto one of the bar stools. "A man who is responsible for my decided lack of sleep. Let me warn you if you haven't made coffee after waking me like that, I'm going to kill you."

"Some friend," Markie said with a scoff. "Threatening me first thing in the morning. But it just so happens that I came here for coffee and since you weren't a good enough hostess to make it, I just made it myself."

"To say I was your hostess would imply I invited you," Babs muttered.

She was wearing a ratty old nightshirt that Markie had bought her years ago. Hot Babe, it proclaimed.

As Babs yawned and pushed back her bed-head dark hair, Markie wondered how long the man who belonged to the boots had been involved with Babs. When a relationship was new, a woman didn't wear ratty pajamas. This couldn't be the first time Babs had been with Mr. Boots.

"You did invite me. The day I moved out, you said I should keep the key and treat the apartment as if it were still mine."

"Well, if it's yours, I can't be the hostess, so stop belly-aching and get me a cup of coffee before I collapse."

"So, who is he?" Markie asked, as she poured a mug of coffee and looked in the direction of the bedroom door.

Babs took the mug and shrugged. "Just some guy."

"Is it serious?" Markie poured herself a mug, then took the bar stool opposite Babs.

"No. Just scratching a mutual itch." Babs sipped the coffee and made a face. "Your mom's coffee is better."

"Yeah, but in order to drink hers you have to be in her vicinity. I decided even good coffee wasn't worth the price. She gave me the *look*."

"What now?" Babs asked.

"Well, she's worried Danny's gay."

Babs choked on her mouthful of coffee. "What?"

"Mom thinks he might be gay. He hasn't dated in a while, so she's worried."

"He's not gay," Babs muttered, taking another sip.

"That's what I told her. And, she's going on about the fact that I found—"

"—and lost a body. Yeah, I heard."

"Bella?"

"No," Babs said. "*My* mom."

Babs was a few years older than Markie, but they'd lived in the neighborhood. A neighborhood that was populated by boys and by prying, nosy mothers.

Markie groaned. "Who needs the Internet when you have the Port Richmond grapevine?"

"So give," Babs said and grimaced as she took a sip of coffee. "What happened?"

"Pretty much what you probably heard. I tripped over a dead body, went in to call 911 from the closet—"

"From the closet?" Babs asked.

"Well, what if the murderer was hiding in the bushes? I didn't want him to find me, so I called from the closet. And by the time the cops got there, it disappeared."

"Speaking of cops," Babs said slowly.

"I'd rather not," Markie muttered, knowing what was coming.

"I also heard something about Zac, you and a dinner at Captain Nemo's?"

Markie sighed. "Yes."

"Mom was so mad she missed the weekly ladies' night out. Finally, something juicy happens and she was nowhere near it. She said she always knew you and Zac were meant to be."

"Meant to be enemies is more like it. He's my least favorite man—after Joel, that is." In the interest of being honest, she added, "And my dead guy. Yes, Zac's definitely number three on my list of most disliked males."

"That's what you say. But sometimes we say things we don't mean."

"Oh, I mean it all right," Markie promised her. "Zac is definitely third on the list."

Suddenly Markie remembered Mr. Zemjek, a truly disagreeable customer who called every week with a new complaint.

"Maybe fourth on the list. But third or fourth, it doesn't matter. Zac's on the least-liked list and odds of him getting off of it are bad, so let's change the subject."

"Fine by me. So what are you doing today?" Babs asked conversationally.

Markie looked at her watch. "I have an appointment over here in twenty minutes. I should probably get going. Are you okay?"

"Yes."

Markie glanced at the boots on the floor and then back at Babs.

"I'm fine," Babs said. "It's nothing serious."

"If you say so. I just don't want to have you hurt again."

Markie'd had one bad experience with Joel. It had been a doozy, no denying that. After all, having your fiancé skip out on the wedding wasn't just hurtful, it was insulting.

Babs had never suffered through that sort of pain, but she still fared pretty badly in the love department. Sometimes quantity counted more than quality, and this was one of those cases.

There was something going on here. Maybe it wasn't just a bed-and-bolt.

"You're sure?" Markie asked.

"Sure," Babs said, offering her a quick smile. "Go. Before you're late."

Markie wasn't satisfied, but she let it lie. Eventually, she'd figure out what was up. "Okay. How about dinner later in the week? Saturday?"

"Sorry, I have plans."

"With Mr. Boots?" Markie asked.

"Yeah," Babs said slowly, as if she didn't want to admit it. She didn't look exactly excited about having plans with Mr. Boots.

"Sunday for lunch then?" Markie pressed, needing to get to the bottom of things.

Babs nodded. "Sounds good."

"Great," Markie said. "I'll pick you up."

"Okay. See you then."

Just then, the shower turned on.

"I could wait and meet him now, if you'd like?" Markie offered.

"No. I don't mean to be rude, but go," Babs said, a sense of urgency in her voice.

"Fine. But you know you'll have to tell me eventually." And eventually would come Sunday afternoon, to be precise.

"Don't worry about my love life," Babs warned her. "Worry about your own."

"I don't have one."

"That's my point. Go."

"Bye."

Babs slammed the door on her.

Markie tromped down the stairs feeling definitely less than better.

Rather than comforted, she had just added to her worries. Dead bodies, Zac Marshall, her mother with the *look* and now something was up with Babs.

Could things get any worse?

Tuesday evening, Zac got out of his car and studied Markie's neighborhood.

Cars and minivans were in driveways and parked curbside. Looked like people were home. Time to ask some questions and maybe get some answers.

He started at the house directly across from Markie's.

He knocked and the door opened, chain still in place, and a woman peeked out.

"Detective Zac Marshall," he said, flashing his badge. "I'd like to ask you a few questions about yesterday morning. There was a man—"

He didn't get any further. The door slammed and he heard the chain rattle before it reopened.

"I can explain," she said, her face pale.

This wasn't the response Zac had expected, but he didn't let his surprise show. "Maybe we should go inside, Miss...?"

"Mrs. Amber Thomas. And I'd rather talk out here, if you don't mind. My husband's inside."

Zac nodded, and pulled out his notepad and jotted down her name. "Now, about yesterday?"

"Paul drove the kids to school. I said I had a doctor's appointment, but I was meeting *him*. I swear I didn't know he was involved with insider trading until I read the paper this morning."

"Him?"

"Don't toy with me, detective. Frank. I didn't plan to get involved with him, but when my aunt left me that money, I wanted to invest it and met Frank."

"And one thing led to another...?"

"Yes," she said. "But I invited him over yesterday morning to break it off, I swear."

A lover's spat. That could explain a lot.

"What did you do with the body?" he asked.

"Body?" There was genuine surprise in her tone and expression. "There was no body. Frank wasn't happy but I told him I loved my husband and couldn't keep cheating. He left, totally alive. Then I read in the paper this morning that he was being investigated."

She paused a moment, then said, "Wait. You think that Markie Walkowicz's disappearing body was Frank? It wasn't. I can give you his number if you need to verify it, but please, don't tell my husband."

Damn. For a moment, he thought he'd solved the case.

Zac took down the information and then asked, "Did you see anything unusual yesterday?"

"Nothing. It's a quiet neighborhood. Frank left and I went to work the lunch at the kids' school."

"Nothing else to add?" he asked, though he held out little hope.

She shook her head.

"Okay, thanks. That's all for now. I'll be in touch if I have any more questions." He turned away.

"You'll keep my secret?" she asked.

"If your story checks out, I will."

"Thank you."

For that one golden moment, he had thought he'd solved the whole thing. But no, that would have been too easy. And nothing involving Markie was ever easy.

Zac tried the next house and met Mrs. Wagner, the mother of four girls.

"Did that Paul next door call in a complaint again?" she asked. Not giving him time to answer she continued, "Because the girls might not be library-quiet, but we're not disturbing the peace."

"No, ma'am," Zac assured her. "It's about your neighbor, Markie Walkowicz."

"Oh, the dead-body girl. Sorry, I can't help you. I didn't see or hear anything."

Zac wasn't surprised. A tank could roll down the street and she'd be hard-pressed to notice with that crew.

Next was Mrs. Wagner's nemesis, Paul Smith, who worked nights and slept days. He hadn't heard anything other than the Wagner girls and wondered if he could file another complaint with Zac as long as he was here.

Zac said no, then tried another house. Margie Dorkowski and her family were all long gone by the time Markie tripped over her body, she assured him.

Sighing, Zac continued down the line of homes across from Markie's.

"Philadelphia police," he said, flashing his badge at an older lady with salt-and-pepper hair.

"You caught me," she said, looking angry rather than scared. "I know I should apologize, but I'm not sorry I dumped that crap. He deserves it."

"Who's he?"

"Don't play games with me, detective. I watch *Law and Order* and I'm aware of all your tricks. He called the health department on my little Muffy last month because she had a tiny little accident on his lawn."

"And so you killed him, then dumped the body?"

"Are you crazy?" she asked. "I took a long walk with Muffy and collected … uh, samples from all over the neighborhood then dumped them on his lawn."

"Gross," Zac said.

"Yeah. Then I called the health department on Paul."

Zac stared at the woman. The entire neighborhood was nuts.

"I'm here about the fact your neighbor across the street found a body on her porch," he said slowly.

"Oh, that," she said, relief in her voice. "I don't know anything about that."

"Of course you don't." Why on earth would the dog-poop-dumping lady worry about a missing corpse when she could worry about her neighborhood feud?

"You can check out my story with the health department," she said.

"I'll just do that. Listen, if you think of anything else, call me," he said, handing her a card.

"Sure."

Zac wanted nothing more than to go home and pop a couple aspirins. More than a couple. But he had one more call to make. Mrs. Gladys Galing, who lived next to Mrs. Sullivan. After that, he was done.

"Detective Zac Marshall," he said, flashing his badge.

"I wondered when you'd get around to questioning me," the older lady grumbled. "Shoddy police work, if you ask me."

She gave him a hard look and then said, "Are you coming in, or does the Philadelphia police force plan on paying my heating bill?"

"Thanks," he said, stepping into the house that smelled like cabbage. It took a bit of effort not to wrinkle his nose at the smell. "About yesterday morning."

"Markie's body."

He nodded, thankful she didn't feel the need to confess any secrets.

"I don't know anything," she said.

"Mind telling me what you were doing yesterday morning?" he asked, needing to verify what he already knew from Mrs. Sullivan.

"I get my hair done every Monday."

"And after that?"

"Why do you need to know what I did after that?"

"It's a routine question, ma'am. I'm just trying to ascertain who does what and when in the neighborhood."

"I don't believe it's any of your business. All you need to know is I was at Bella's beauty salon when Markie found her body. I have an alibi. You can check it out."

Something wasn't right here.

"How about the night before?" he asked, hoping for something more to go on.

"I was here, alone. No witnesses. But about Monday, you can check with Bella."

"I'll do that," he said.

"Well, that's all I have to say," she said abruptly.

Zac allowed himself to be shooed out the door. What was up in Markie's *quiet* neighborhood?

Quietly insane, that's what it was.

Markie's disappearing corpse suddenly seemed like the most normal thing that had happened on the street this week

By Friday, Zac had checked out everyone's stories. He'd talked with everyone from housewives to health department workers.

He had no one left to check except a certain Mrs. Randolph, who'd left town Monday to take care of her sick mother, according to her husband. He'd called Mrs. Randolph's mother's house, but rather than a quiet sick room, he heard the distinct sounds of a crowd in the background.

He didn't think that was much of a lead. Given the odd stories in the neighborhood the woman probably had a totally logical—albeit insane—explanation.

He still hadn't heard anything from Markie.

And he didn't exactly expect to.

Oh, he hoped, but he'd been hoping for eleven months and look where that had gotten him.

Nowhere.

Maybe if the mother contingent hadn't descended on them at that particular moment, they might have said some of the things that needed to be said.

The meal had been going well, up to that point. Better than he thought it could.

But the moment was ruined and Markie had run out.

It would have been polite if she'd at least called to thank him for dropping off her cake. It had been a harrowing experience.

He had opened the door to her office expecting to see her and found ... her mother.

Yes, dropping off her cake and dealing with her mother certainly warranted a call of thanks.

But it didn't look as if he was going to hear from Markie. Maybe it was time she heard from him.

Damn.

"Problems?" Manning, standing next to Zac's desk smirking, asked.

Zac realized he must have spoken aloud.

"No. No problems."

"You're sure?" Manning shot him a sly look. "My aunt said you and the crazy chick went out to dinner."

"Markie's not crazy."

"Seeing dead bodies? That's not quite sane."

If Zac had been asked last week, he'd have said Manning seemed like an okay sort of cop. But that wouldn't be his answer if asked today.

"Watch it, Manning," he warned.

"Maybe if Walkowicz had watched it, we'd have found a body. But instead, she crawled into the closet to call 911. Rather than a closet, I think she needs a nice padded cell."

"Manning."

Generally, the warning in his tone was enough to convince anyone they'd gone too far. Even someone who didn't know him well knew it was time to be quiet when he spoke like this. But obviously, Manning wasn't all that bright. He kept right on talking. "Don't worry, big guy. I won't let it be known around the station that you have a thing for crazy chicks."

"Do worry, patrolman. If I hear another word about Markie from you. Anything."

"Or what?" Manning asked, that damned smirk still plastered on his face.

Zac stood, towering over the patrolman. "Or I'll have a talk with your supervisor and you'll find yourself on crossing guard duty for the rest of the school term."

"You wouldn't," Manning said, no smirk on his face this time, as he craned his neck to look Zac in the eye. Whatever he saw there made him visibly pale.

Zac looked down at the new patrolman. He'd never make it on the force if he didn't learn that sometimes discretion was the better part of valor.

"Watch me," he said.

Manning shrugged and tried to look nonchalant, though he didn't quite pull it off. "Whatever. I've heard a lot about you, but I've never heard you were such a tightass."

"Then obviously you haven't heard enough."

Manning stomped away.

Zac sat back down at his desk, picked up the phone and dialed Markie's number for about the twentieth time since Monday. This time he didn't hang up, but waited for the answering machine to pick up.

"Hey, Markie. It's Zac. Wondered if you'd like to do something this weekend. Call me. The number's still the same."

He hung up and felt like a fool.

She wasn't going to call him back.

And though he'd like to think he wouldn't call her again, odds were that he would.

Women.

They made him crazy.

5

Saturday had been a blur of activity for Markie that ended in her bathing Mrs. Flynn's old English mastiff. She'd wanted nothing more than to come home and crawl into a big bubble bath to wash the stench of wet dog off. Two hundred pounds of wet dog.

Ugh.

But her hopes of a bubble bath faded when, the minute she pulled into a parking space, she saw Mrs. Randolph amble across the street with something in her hand.

"Markie," she yoohooed.

"Hi, Mrs. Randolph."

"I brought you a casserole."

"You did?" Markie looked at the covered baking dish, puzzled.

"I make my four-layer casserole for all the funerals."

"But there hasn't been a death in my family."

"No, but I just got home today and heard there was a body on your porch, so I thought it was appropriate."

"Thanks," she said, not knowing what else to say as her neighbor thrust the casserole into her hands.

"Now, about the body," Mrs. Randolph said.

"Yes?"

"Mr. Randolph said there's been a cop asking questions."

"A detective."

"He even called my mother to check out my story," she said. "I mean, do I need an alibi? Am I a suspect?"

"Not as far as I know," Markie assured her. "They're not really sure they believe I saw a body, so I don't think there's a suspect list. Why? Should you be?"

"Well, of course not. I'm a member of the Rosary Committee. I don't go around hiding dead bodies. It's just that I left suddenly that day. My mother was sick. I didn't want that officer—"

"Detective," Markie corrected. She remembered when Zac made detective. He'd been so pleased. She'd taken him to Nemo's and celebrated.

She tucked the memory away and concentrated on her casserole-carrying neighbor.

"Well, I mean, my mother said I was with her, and I was, but if he checks further he'll find she wasn't really sick like I told my husband. We were in Atlantic City."

"Why did you lie to your husband?"

"He doesn't approve of gambling. I mean, I tell him that some churches have bingo, but he says that's different. It's money going to God, not to the mob. But every now and again, Mom and I take a few days. I made five hundred dollars. Blackjack. I've got a method."

"I'm sure if you tell that to the detective, he can check out your story and he won't tell your husband, although I think honesty is probably the best policy between a husband and a wife."

Mrs. Randolph laughed. "I can tell you've never been married, sweetie. Take it from me, sometimes a good lie can be the best thing you can do for your relationship."

"But—"

"Listen, would you just see to it that your detective comes over to talk to me after my husband's gone to work?"

"Sure. I'll let him know."

"Thanks, Markie. And not a word of this to anyone."

"My lips are sealed."

Markie watched Mrs. Randolph hurry back across the street and then carried her casserole into the house.

A quick bath, then four-layer casserole.

Maybe things were looking up?

Markie woke up Sunday to the sound of the telephone giving one last half ring before the answering machine picked up.

She had the volume turned way down so she couldn't hear who was calling, although she suspected she knew anyway.

She'd had two persistent callers all week—Zac and her mother.

Odds were it was one of them.

And she didn't want to talk to either of them.

She glanced at the clock. It was almost noon.

She groaned.

She hadn't slept well last night, despite the bubble bath and delicious casserole. Actually, she hadn't slept well since Monday.

Dreams plagued her sleep.

Dreams of dead bodies on the porch … and of Zac.

Dreams of dead bodies in the living room … and of Zac.

Dreams of her mother nagging her to be a teacher … and of Zac.

There was one particular nightmare that featured her wedding day. Her mother was standing next to her, telling her that now that she was getting married, she should become a teacher. As Markie looked down the aisle, it wasn't Joel walking toward her, but rather Zac, in an orange and green plaid suit.

The sight should have been horrifying, instead, she'd smiled in her dreams.

Smiled at Zac.

Suddenly, they weren't in the church any longer. They were in her old treehouse and Zac reached out and touched her face, gently, tenderly, almost like a lover as he whispered her name ... *Markie.*

All her dreams were disturbing, but it was the last one that was the worst.

It wasn't Zac in the horrible suit, it was him touching her so softly, and her ... liking it. After all, she'd never had feelings like that for Zac.

Markie knew she had to shake off these horrible nightmares. She was so thankful she'd made arrangements to spend the day with Babs.

They'd talk about the mysterious Mr. Boots and get Markie's mind off her weird dreams.

She took a shower, dressed and thought about making breakfast, but decided to wait until she got Babs. Maybe they'd go to the small diner down the street for eggs. Heck, it was lunchtime. Maybe they'd get big, juicy hamburgers.

She slipped on her shoes and opened the front door cautiously.

It had become her habit to peek out before stepping onto the porch. She didn't think she could stand tripping on a corpse again. Or dealing with another neighbor.

The coast was clear. She pulled her jacket tight against the brutal cold wind.

"Markie?"

She groaned. The coast most definitely was not clear.

She pasted a smile on her face and turned to her neighbor. "Hi, Mrs. Sullivan."

"Dear, I just wanted to check on you. I can't believe all the goings-on in our quiet little neighborhood."

"Yes, it was a trying week, but I'm fine."

"Are you sure? I mean, that one officer has been nosing around here every day since."

Markie shrugged. "Well, I think we've seen the last of him."

"Are you sure, dear? I mean, he seemed rather persistent."

She thought of the phone that had rung earlier. She'd left the light blinking away, message untouched. Maybe it was Zac. But it could have been her mom, or Danny, or just about anyone.

Just because someone called on a Sunday morning, it didn't mean it was Zac.

"Even the most persistent person has to admit defeat eventually. He couldn't find a body, so there's nothing more he can do."

"Well, that's good. There's something nerve-racking about having the police around so much. Now, you run along. I'd better get in before all my heat gets out."

"I'll see you later, Mrs. Sullivan," Markie said, shutting the door succinctly.

Markie's stomach growled as she climbed the stairs to Babs's. That hamburger was sounding better and better. Nice greasy hamburgers with Babs.

Markie practically sprinted up the rest of the apartment stairs. She knocked once and then unlocked the door.

"Babs," she called as she let herself in.

No answer.

Her friend slept like the dead. Markie figured that was the other good part of Babs working freelance … she was never late for work.

"We had a date. Come on, get up. I'm starving. I can't believe you're still sleeping at almost one o'clock in the afternoon."

Markie threw open the bedroom door and then slammed it again.

Babs had been curled up in her bed with someone ... someone who looked decidedly like Markie's baby brother.

Oh.

Ick.

Her brother.

Her baby brother.

Her baby brother was Mr. Boots?

Markie felt nauseous.

She should go before they came out.

Danny and Babs?

Oh, man. Thank goodness they'd only been sleeping.

As it was, she wished she could bleach the image out of her mind. Because her brother cuddled next to Babs was more than enough information.

Thank goodness it was cold enough for covers. If she'd walked in on them in the heat of summer.

Oh.

Ick.

She should leave. The situation was just downright embarrassing.

Her brother and her best friend.

And what would her mother say when she found out Danny had a girlfriend?

Suddenly, despite the lingering embarrassment, she smiled. Her mother would be thrilled.

She'd be dancing on the ceiling with joy.

Heck, the fact Danny was with a good Polish girl would be a bonus.

Danny, dating someone from the neighborhood? Maybe her mother would forget Markie wasn't a teacher and saw dead bodies, and concentrate on marrying off Danny and Babs.

She should hurry and get out before either of them walked out the door.

She started toward the front door and then heard the bedroom door open.

Too late.

"Hi, sis," Danny said as he nonchalantly walked into the kitchen area, took the coffee carafe and filled it with water.

He'd put on shorts and a T-shirt, for which Markie would be eternally grateful.

"*Hi, sis?*" she repeated. "That's all you have to say to me?"

He turned and shot her a grin. "How about if I add, *Hi, sis… knock next time would you?* Is that better?"

She could feel her face warm and she began to babble nervously, "I can't tell you how sorry I am. I would have, but we had arranged to go out, so Babs was expecting me. I'm used to walking in and waking her up, unless she's actively dating, but it's been a long time since she's had a man, and there were no boots in the living room."

"Boots in the living room?" he asked. "Is that like a tie on the doorknob?"

"No. It's just the other day your boots were out here and—"

"Babs told you about us?" he asked, looking at her intently.

"No," Markie said slowly. "She wouldn't tell me who Mr. Boots was. I figured I'd worm it out of her today."

Danny frowned. She couldn't tell what he was thinking, but he didn't look pleased.

"What's going on?" she asked.

"Nothing," he said, his voice practically a growl.

"Really, what?"

"Really, that's what's going on … absolutely nothing." He raked his hand through his short brown hair. "Babs won't tell anyone."

"Tell them what?"

"About us. More specifically, about me."

"Why?" Markie asked. It had been a bit of a shock to find Babs and Danny together, but now that she'd had a moment to adjust her universe to that reality, the idea of them together was growing on her.

Her best friend and her brother? What could be better? Plus, Danny and Babs would *definitely* take up a lot of her mother's interest, which would leave Markie off the hook.

"Why?" Babs said as she walked out of the bedroom. "Because it's no one's business. Did you want something, Markie?"

"We had a date, remember?"

"No," Babs said with a quick glance at Danny. "No, I guess I didn't."

Danny was glaring at Babs, who went from glancing to glaring right back at him.

At least no one was glaring at her, but Markie felt awkward nonetheless. "Listen, no problem. I'll just go. Call me later if you want to talk. I'm so sorry for barging in on the two of you."

She headed for the door.

"Markie?" Babs asked.

Markie stopped. "Yeah?"

"You're not going to tell anyone, are you?"

"Not if you don't want me to," she promised.

"I don't," Babs said.

Danny slammed the filter into the coffee maker and without a word stalked into the bedroom. He returned carrying his boots and a pile of clothes as he headed for the door.

"Danny, are you mad at me?" Markie asked.

"Not you," he said. He opened the door and turned back to look at Babs. "Don't call me. I mean it this time. Don't call me unless you're ready to take our relationship public. I'm tired of keeping this a secret."

Babs moved toward him, but he pulled back. "Danny, we've been over all the reasons why we should keep this just between us."

"No. You've been over all the reasons. I've given you the one reason why we should. I love you. And I think, if you'd let yourself, you'd realize you love me."

"I do care about you," Babs said. "That's why—"

"Save it. Save the excuses. Save it all. Call me when you're ready, but not before."

He walked out, slamming the door behind him.

Babs sank onto the couch and sniffed.

"Do you want me to go?" Markie asked.

"No . . . ." Babs said, drawing the word out until it hitched in her throat.

"Honey," Markie said, sitting next to her friend. "What's going on?"

"I think Danny's right."

"Right about?"

"I think I love him." Her declaration held no happiness. As a matter of fact, it was almost a wail of despair.

"That's wonderful. Why, he just said he loved you. You love him. It's perfect."

Markie could already see it. Danny and Babs at the altar. She'd be the maid of honor.

The old maid.

The one her mother would wince about to her friends. *My daughter, Markie. I begged her to be a teacher and marry some nice Polish boy. But no, she just had to be a single handyman who trips over dead bodies.*

Dead bodies made her think of Zac.

And she had a brief flashback to last night's most disturbing dream. Zac walking down the aisle toward her. Only this time, he wasn't wearing a plaid suit. He was in a tux and he was smiling—

"Perfect?" Babs squawked, pulling Markie from her fantasy. "It's perfectly awful."

Markie had to agree...all these fantasies about Zac Marshall were perfectly awful. But she didn't voice her agreement, instead she tried to focus on Babs's turmoil.

Plus, Mom's worried that he's gay and has been looking for men to set him up with. She'll be so ecstatic he's dating she probably won't bother you at all...well, hardly at all."

"But don't you see, I love him so I can't be with him."

"I don't get it," Markie said, feeling more than a bit thick.

"I'm a relationship nightmare. Totally toxic. In the past, I've dated men who weren't looking for longterm anything. Losers. It didn't matter."

"But Danny matters?" Markie asked.

Babs sniffed loudly and nodded.

"Maybe that's why all the other relationships failed. They didn't matter. The guys were losers. I'll vouch for that. But Danny...he's different. You're different with him. You love him. You've never said that about any of the other guys."

"You can't tell anyone," she said.

"But—"

"Promise."

Markie crossed her heart. "Fine. I promise I won't tell anyone you're dating Danny."

Babs stared at the apartment door. "After the way he left here today, it might not matter anyway. I've never seen him so mad."

"Sure you have. You remember the time we tried to fix him up with ... what was her name? Laurel? He needed a date for the prom, and we thought they'd be perfect together."

Babs gave a weak smile. "Unfortunately, her boyfriend didn't see it that way."

"Yeah. Danny was easily angrier then than he was today. Why not just come out of the closet? You've never hidden boyfriends away before, have you?"

Babs shook her head. "No."

"Why not just let everyone know you're dating Danny? I'll deny it if you ever tell him, but truth be told, my baby brother is a catch."

Babs blew her nose. "Your baby brother. That's just it. You realize I'm turning thirty? I'm two years older than you and he's your baby brother. Thirty. I'll be thirty."

Markie simply nodded.

"I'll be thirty and he'll be twenty-five. That's almost half a decade separating us."

"Come on, he'll be twenty-six next month. Four years. That's nothing. I think I have leftovers in my refrigerator that are older than that."

"I've never dated a younger man," Babs admitted.

"So?"

"What will people think?" Babs wailed.

"Since *when* does Betty Ann Kreszewski worry about what anyone thinks?"

"Since now, I guess," she said.

"Well, stop," Markie said, a mock stern command.

Babs managed a weak smile. "Stop worrying? Just like that. Well, that's easy for you to say. Zac's older than you are."

"What does Zac have to do with this?" Markie asked.

Suddenly the tables were turned. Babs's eyes narrowed and she studied Markie a moment, then said, "You tell me."

"Nothing. Zac has nothing to do with this discussion, or with me."

"Sure. Tell it to someone who doesn't know you like I do," Babs said with a laugh. "There have always been sparks between the two of you."

"The only sparks you've seen are the ones caused by his overbearing, thinks-he-knows-it-all attitude. Look how he chased Joel away."

"Markie, no matter what you say, I know you don't believe that. I've never quite figured out why you were so furious with Zac about the whole wedding disaster."

"Zac tried to warn me off Joel, and when he couldn't, he talked Joel out of marrying me."

"I don't think he did—we both heard about Joel and that stripper. He was seen all over town with her before they took off for Vegas together. But even if Zac did try to talk Joel out of marrying you—well, why do you think he'd do that?"

"I—"

Markie had asked herself many questions since the big wedding-that-wasn't. Some of those questions had to do with how she'd ever let herself think she was in love with a slug like Joel. Some had to do with how she ever imagined she was friends with someone like Zac. But none had ever concerned why Zac might have tried to stop the wedding.

"He cared about you," Babs said. "I think he still does."

"As a friend maybe."

"Markie, maybe I should have said something sooner, but I didn't think you were ready. I've seen Zac watching you … it wasn't just friendly."

Markie shook her head. "No way."

"He wanted you."

"No."

"Oh, yes. And I don't think that wanting has gone away."

"But, he's my friend. Was my friend."

"Can you say that about Joel? That he was ever your friend?"

"No."

"So maybe that's what was wrong. Maybe there has to be more than a physical attraction. Maybe there has to be friendship as well."

Markie was feeling decidedly uncomfortable, so she turned the tables again. "What about you and Danny? Is there friendship there?"

"Yes. That's where it started. With friendship. After that dinner at your mom and dad's last month, he drove me home, remember?"

Markie and Babs had gone to her parents' together, Danny had taken Babs home while Markie stayed and helped her mom with the broken garbage disposal. "Yeah, I remember."

"We went to a movie together, and ... well ..."

"Friendship led to more."

"Yes," Babs said, sounding dejected. "Listen, can we talk about something else?"

Markie nodded. She didn't mind the talking-about-Danny-and-Babs part of the conversation, but the whole analyzing-Zac part was making her decidedly nervous.

"Sounds good. No more talk of men. Let's talk hamburgers around the corner. I'm starving."

"Give me five minutes to get dressed."

Yes, meat was so much easier to talk about than men.

6

By Monday morning, Zac was in a foul mood.

It had been one week since he'd gone to Markie's house for the 5292.

Since then, he'd left six—count them, six—messages on Markie's answering machine, wanting to update her on the investigation, although there wasn't much to say.

Nothing to say, as a matter of fact—at least nothing about the investigation.

There was a lot to say about her seemingly quiet, normal neighborhood.

Cheating spouses, dog-poop-dumping ladies, loud little girls and the mysterious whereabouts of Mrs. Gladys Galing, who did indeed have a hair appointment every Monday in preparation for meeting her mystery man, according to Bella at the salon.

Then there was Mrs. Randolph, who had left last Monday to take care of her *sick* mother. He'd made some calls and her mother wasn't sick...and wasn't at home either.

Other than that, everyone else checked out. That's why he'd left those six messages, just to tell Markie that. It was business.

He wasn't going to count the umpteen times he'd dialed her number and hung up.

That didn't count.

Every time he swore that was it, that he was done trying to talk to her, to explain things.

He'd hold out as long as he could, picking up the phone to call her and then slamming it back down. Until finally, one time he'd forgotten to slam the receiver down and he'd talked to her stupid machine again.

He knew her message by heart. *Hi. You've reached Markie Walkowicz. You know what to do.* Short and to the point. Although it worried him that she gave her name on the machine. She was practically advertising she was a woman who lived alone.

Maybe he'd convince her to let him record a new message if she ever called him back. If she ever agreed to see him.

He was done waiting for her to get over that stupid Walkowicz grudge thing. He was going over to her place after work and, like it or not, she was going to listen to him.

Decision made, he pulled up in front of the station. He'd just shut off the engine when his cell phone rang.

He glanced at the screen.

Markie's number.

"Took you long enough to call me back," he said as he picked up. "I want to try another dinner. Somewhere out of the way where no one we know can find us. We'll—"

"Zac," she interrupted. "I didn't call about dinner. I called because it's back."

"What's back?" he asked.

"The body. It's in the backyard this time, not on the porch, but it's the same corpse. No one else would own a suit that ugly. Can you get over here right away? I'm going to head back outside in case it tries to disappear again. I'll be in the back."

"Markie, don't go out. Lock your door."

She disconnected the phone.

Zac cursed as he started the car back up and backed out of his parking space.

The crazy woman was outside in her backyard watching a corpse.

Last time, she was so afraid that there was a murderer hiding in the bushes that she'd hid in the closet. This time, she was babysitting the body.

Zac knew that at this time of day, with all the morning traffic, it was going to take him at least fifteen minutes to get to her neighborhood. That was just too damned long. Anything could happen to her in fifteen minutes.

He got on the radio.

"Dispatch, I need you to send a unit to..." He gave them Markie's address and tried to think of a reason to give without using the 5292 code. Finally, he just said, "Tell them to go out back and wait for me."

The dispatcher came back on a few seconds later and said a unit had been sent.

The knot in Zac's gut relaxed a little, but he knew it wouldn't totally dissipate until he saw for himself that Markie was all right.

The drive was the longest fifteen minutes of his life.

He'd pictured all the things that could happen to Markie out there. None of them did anything to relieve his anxiety.

Zac screeched to a halt in front of her house and ran into the back.

Markie stood in the middle of the backyard.

She didn't smile when she spotted him. Didn't frown, either. She just looked blank.

"Markie?" he asked gently.

"It was gone again."

"Gone?"

"When I came back out here after I called you, it was gone. Then Manning showed up. How could you send him?"

Damn. He should have told dispatch to send anyone but Manning. "I didn't send him. I just asked dispatch to send a car. I didn't want you out here alone. Whatever's going on, it's not good. You should have waited in the house."

"I didn't want it to disappear again. I mean, I was only in the house a couple minutes. How could it disappear so fast?"

He scanned the yard and saw nothing—absolutely nothing—out of the ordinary. "You're sure you saw it? You weren't just dreaming and thought you saw it?"

She gave him a disgusted look. "I know what I saw. Are you going to laugh, too? I thought Manning was going to wet his pants, he was laughing so hard. He just turned around and walked back to his car. He's officially on my least-liked list."

"I'm not laughing." But he was going to kick Manning's ass. The kid should have waited for him to get here before leaving Markie.

She looked at him and sighed. "No, you're not laughing. Thanks. I appreciate that."

She looked so lost and confused. Zac wanted nothing more than to put his arms around her and hug her, to make everything safe again. But he knew she'd probably slug him, so he settled for saying, "Let's look around and see if we can find any clues."

She shot him a look of gratitude. "Thanks."

They walked the perimeter of the yard, side by side. The only thing Zac saw were their little puffs of breath in the cold Philly morning air.

The small yard wasn't fenced. There was nothing really to mark its perimeter. None of the backyards of any of the houses on this block were fenced. The only boundary was a small shed.

Markie stopped in front of it and froze. "Hey, look." There was excitement in her voice.

She knelt down.

Zac joined her and spotted a small piece of fabric.

She reached for it.

"Don't touch it," Zac warned.

He studied it.

Green and orange plaid.

It couldn't be a coincidence that they'd found fabric that matched Markie's description of what the body had been wearing.

There had been a corpse in Markie's backyard.

A corpse wearing an orange and green plaid suit.

Zac hadn't exactly doubted her, but he hadn't exactly believed her either.

Now he had proof and a chill crept up his spine. Something was going on and Markie was somehow in the middle of it.

"What's in the shed?"

"The only thing Mrs. Sullivan, Mrs. Galing and I use it for is the lawn mower and a few yard tools. I don't keep my personal tools in there. And we haven't used the mower in months and thankfully, despite the cold, we haven't had any snow that even warranted the shovel."

It had been a cold winter so far, sinking the city into a deep freeze, but all the major snowstorms had blown right by them.

Most of the time, no snow was a good thing, but what Zac wouldn't give for even a coating right now. Snow would mean tracks. Tracks might give him answers. But the frozen-solid ground left him nothing but a small piece of fabric to go with.

"Do you know the combination to the lock?" Zac asked.

"Sure." She started to stand, as if she were going to unlock it, but Zac put a hand on her shoulder.

"No. I'll do it. Just tell me the combination, then stand back."

Markie did, and for once, obeyed him without question.

He twirled the lock, then nodded to the side. "Over there," he said, drawing his weapon. He kicked the door open.

Markie had been right. The only thing the small shed contained was a lawn mower, a small red plastic gas can and a few shovels and rakes.

Zac stepped back outside and scanned the backyard. He had to have missed something. But as far as he could tell, the only thing here was the small square of cloth.

"Come on. Let's go to my car for an evidence bag."

"No," she said, kneeling back down by the square of cloth.

"What do you mean, no? I'm not leaving you back here when we don't know what's going on."

"And I'm not leaving the only clue we've got. What if it disappears, too? No, I'll just watch it until you're back. Plus, what could happen? We've checked the yard and the shed. No one's here."

His car was parked in the drive. Markie would only be out of his sight for a few seconds.

He could either just pick up the cloth and destroy any potential evidence, or he could make a run for an evidence bag.

She was right. There was no one living or dead back here.

"Fine," he said. "Don't touch it. And if anyone comes into the backyard, scream before they get close. I mean, even if it's someone you know."

"I won't touch the cloth, and I promise to holler if anyone, living or dead, shows up."

Not exactly satisfied, but out of options, Zac sprinted to his car. He grabbed an evidence bag and gloves, then ran back into the yard, nervous about leaving her alone for even a minute. His chest felt constricted until he spotted her and he could breathe again.

Markie was staring at the scrap of cloth, as if she was afraid to even blink in case it disappeared.

Zac slipped on a glove, picked up the cloth and put it in a small plastic bag.

"There," he said, pulling the glove back off. He stuffed the evidence bag into his inner jacket pocket.

He offered her a hand up, and was surprised when she took it. Her hand was a block of ice. The light canvas work jacket she was wearing wasn't nearly thick enough for this kind of weather.

"Don't lose it," Markie warned.

"I won't."

"So now what?" she asked.

"Why don't you go inside and warm up and I'll canvass the neighborhood again on the off chance someone else saw something. But if last Monday is any indication, I don't think we're going to have a lot of luck finding anyone home. Mondays, it seems, the neighborhood is deserted."

"Actually, I shouldn't have been home now. I left, then realized I'd forgotten my pipe wrench. It's in my mudroom. I went in to grab it, and that's when I saw the body."

"So you'd left to go to work, but then came back unexpectedly?" Zac asked.

So whoever was moving the corpse around thought the coast was clear. Markie had left. Everyone else was gone, and Markie's elderly neighbor was parked in front of the television watching her morning show.

Then Markie returned and spotted the body.

Last week, she'd been late for work. So maybe this week, they waited until she actually left, then went to retrieve the body and … and what?

What the hell was going on?

"Yes. I was only gone about fifteen minutes. I pulled in the drive, went in through the front of the house."

"Why not go right into the back?"

"There's a dead bolt on the back door. I don't have a key. So I went through the front of the house. I walked straight to the mudroom. I heard a noise, I think. A small bang, maybe. Not like a gun, but something slamming. Anyway, I looked out the window and there he was. Again."

Zac needed to think about this. But first he needed to see if anyone else saw anything. He'd start with Mrs. Sullivan.

"Okay, go on in the house and wait for me," he said.

"No way. I'm going with you."

"Markie—"

She gave him a look. It was the kind of look his mother used on him. The kind of look he knew Markie's mother had used with her. It was a look that said, "I'm not taking any crap from you." It was a look that any woman who grew up in their Port Richmond section of Philadelphia had perfected by the age of six.

"Markie," he said again.

"Don't you Markie me, Zachary Marshall." She waggled a finger at him.

First, the look; then, a finger waggle.

Zac waggled back and tried to shoot her a look, but knew even his well-practiced cop look couldn't compete with a Port Richmond woman look. "Don't you Zachary me, Marquette Ann Walkowicz."

"Fine. But there's nothing you can do. I'm coming with you…" she paused a moment and whispered, "Zachary."

He didn't know whether to laugh or strangle her.

Trading gibes felt almost like old times, and despite the mystery of the disappearing body, he felt more upbeat than he had since dinner last Monday.

He walked toward the front of her house and didn't argue anymore when she joined him. Actually, having her with him meant that if the body turned up again, he'd be there when she spotted it.

Yes, keeping Markie close was probably a good idea.

His body tightened as he thought about just how close he'd like to keep her. He pictured his mother and hers giving him a *look* of disapproval and the tightening eased immediately.

The look could kill sexual desire instantly.

Zac headed straight to Mrs. Sullivan's and knocked.

She opened the door, a smile pasted on her face. "Oh, you two startled me. No one ever knocks on my door on Mondays." She looked at them a moment and then asked, "Is there a problem?"

"Can we come in a moment?" Zac asked.

"I don't have time for visitors. I have an appointment at Manchester Seniors' Home."

"We'll only take a moment of your time," Zac assured her.

Mrs. Sullivan, her reluctance evident, allowed them both in before shutting the door.

"Now, what's this all about?" she asked.

"Did you notice anything this morning? Anything out of the ordinary?" Zac asked.

"Nothing unusual. This is a quiet neighborhood," she paused a moment, looked at Markie and added, "At least, it was a quiet and orderly neighborhood until recently."

"Not quite as orderly as you'd think," Zac muttered.

"Markie, dear, you know I was your grandmother's best friend for years, and I've loved having you next door, but really, honey, I think it's time to admit there's something wrong. And I don't think it's a body ... I think it's you. Maybe you should see a doctor?"

"Mrs. Sullivan, there was a body. I have proof—"

Zac interrupted by clearing his throat loudly, then started coughing loudly.

He didn't want Markie telling anyone about the cloth. At least not yet.

He saw that Markie understood because she dropped her *proof* talk and patted his back as he faked choking.

"You didn't see or hear anything?" he asked.

"No. Now if you don't mind, I have to leave."

"Well, thanks, Mrs. Sullivan," he said, ushering Markie out the door.

"Are we going to talk to other neighbors?"

Zac didn't like how pale Markie was looking. Pale and cold. Maybe it was shock.

"I doubt anyone will be in. I'll go knock on a few doors on my way out and come back later and do a more thorough job. Maybe someone saw something on their way out to work. Let's get you inside."

He opened her door. It was unlocked. He'd better give the house a once-over before he left. He hated not knowing what was going on and having Markie living alone in the midst of it.

What if she was right? What if someone thought she knew too much?

"I'm checking the house," he announced and did a hurried walk-through before she could argue.

But Markie still seemed a bit out of it ... she didn't even utter a peep of protest.

The house was clear.

Relieved, he joined her in the living room. She was simply sitting on the couch. He wanted to wrap her in his arms, but he simply sat with his thigh brushing hers, trying to be satisfied with the slight contact.

Zac tried to blot the picture that was trying to form from his mind.

He concentrated on Markie. She looked a little warmer now. There was color back in her cheeks. A stray strand of hair had fallen forward and without thinking, he brushed it back in place.

She looked startled and slid a fraction of an inch farther away from him.

"So now what do we do?" she asked.

Zac wanted to say, *I take you in my arms and kiss you until you forget all about any man who came before me.* Instead, he settled for asking, "Are you going in to work today? You could probably use a day off."

"I don't take many days off. And I can't today. I have appointments."

Actually, it was probably better that she was out of the neighborhood, out of the house where anything could happen.

All sorts of different scenarios ran through Zac's mind. None of which he liked.

No way was Markie staying here alone.

He had a plan. She wouldn't like it, but she'd simply have to learn to live with it ... to live with him. He was moving in until they figured out just what was going on.

"What time are you done?" he asked.

"I don't know. Four-ish?"

He nodded, then stood. "Fine. I'll meet you back here. I'll even bring a pizza."

"You don't have to—"

"Sure I do. I'll take care of dinner tonight, you take care of it tomorrow. While we're rooming together, we'll split the cooking and cleaning duties fifty-fifty."

He was rather impressed by how he'd slid that into the conversation.

Markie didn't look nearly as impressed as she jumped from the couch. "Rooming together? We're not rooming together."

Zac stood and faced her. "Sure we are. At least until we figure out what's going on. Now, let's get your pipe wrench and I'll walk you to your car."

"Zac, you're not moving in—"

He watched her, sputtering and gesticulating and before he knew it, he did it.

He kissed her.

Oh, he'd kissed Markie before. Brotherly little pecks on the cheeks here and there throughout their friendship.

But this wasn't brotherly.

Not by a long shot.

He simply reached out, swept her into his arms and silenced her argument by putting his lips on hers. Since she was in the middle of a sentence, her lips were conveniently parted and Zac took advantage of it, deepening what otherwise might have been a chaste kiss.

There was nothing chaste about his exploration of Markie's lips, of her mouth. He tightened his arms around her, pulling her as close as he could, cursing the fact they both still had on jackets, wishing it were summer and that they were barely clothed.

Thinking of Markie wearing next to nothing led to an immediate follow-up thought of Markie wearing absolutely nothing, and even thoughts of his mother giving him *the look* weren't enough to stem the tightening below his waist.

He groaned, and knowing that he was moments away from scooping her up and carrying her into her room, he pushed himself away from her.

When he took Markie to her room—something he planned to do as soon as possible—he wanted to make sure she wanted it as much as he did.

Today, she was traumatized and scared. He wouldn't take advantage of those facts to get what he wanted. Okay, so he'd taken advantage of it in order to move in and protect her. But when it came to making love to Markie, he wasn't going to use her mental upset against her. He'd waited years for his chance, and he could wait a while longer, even if it killed him.

He looked at her standing there, her lips slightly swollen from his kiss. Waiting, being a gentleman, might very well do him in.

Before he could change his mind, he took another step back and said, "So then I'll see you here tonight about four."

"But—" Markie said, looking dazed. No trace of paleness remained. She had a nice rosy pink tint to her cheeks.

Zac glanced at the mirror over Markie's fireplace and gave himself *the look*. It didn't have the same wilting effect as his mother's look would, but it did help him get himself back in control.

"Come on, let's go," he said gently.

"Listen, you can't just… Well, I won't have … You're not moving in."

She fumed, but Zac ignored her. He was actually whistling by the time he got her packed into her car and on her way.

Something was going on here.

And it wasn't just a disappearing dead body.

No. It was more.

A certain chemistry between him and Markie was definitely there.

He'd tried to convince himself it was just some remnant of a childhood crush, but it was more. So much more.

He was anxious to move in and see just what sort of chemical reaction resulted.

7

Markie fumed all day.

Moving in?

Zac kissed her like she hadn't been kissed in months.

Actually, if she was honest, she couldn't remember ever having been kissed like that.

It was a kiss that was one step away from sex.

She'd always thought kissing was nice. Sometimes it was hot.

But this wasn't just hot. It was sizzling.

Zac had practically kissed her socks off, making her forget everything, then he abruptly pulled away and told her he was moving in.

Heavy-handed dork.

Zac thought just like that he could move in with her?

Yeah, that was just what she needed—someone from her least-liked list hanging around all day and all night.

The thoughts of Zac in her house all night made her stomach twist. Probably the beginnings of an ulcer.

If he thought kissing her like that could get him off her list and into her bed … well, it couldn't. It wouldn't even get him into her guest room if she wasn't a bit nervous about her missing dead body.

She tried to think about the people on her least-liked list to get her mind off how thin the wall between her room and the guest room was.

Joel.

The dead body.

Zac.

Oh, and Manning.

Yeah, Manning was soooo on her list.

Actually, even though she was annoyed with Zac for not only kissing her, but also for thinking he had the right to just move in, Manning was still higher on her list.

Joel.

The body.

Manning.

Oh, and there was Mr. Zemjek, her pain-in-the-butt client, and Sylvia Carson, who had once commented on her big feet back in high school. Yes, she'd almost forgotten that there were females on her list.

Mr. Zemjek and Sylvia came after Manning.

Then Zac.

She was going to forget about the body, forget about men in general—both living and missing dead ones—and she was most especially going to forget about kisses that melted her to mush.

She was going to concentrate on work.

Markie stormed into her office, waltzed over to the answering machine and hit the play button, hoping for some big, would-take-all-her-time-and-energy sort of job.

"Message number one," the machine said in its monotone voice.

"Markie, this is your mother. *How could you?* Seeing a body once was bad enough. But twice? If you'd only been a teacher—"

Markie deleted the rest of her mother's lament.

Oh, yeah, Manning was higher on her list than Zac. And he was working on higher than even the disappearing body.

"Message number two."

"Markie, it's Zac Marshall." Like she wouldn't know? "Just thought I'd give you a heads-up … the news is out and about. Mom just called. See you tonight. Oh, and why don't you stop and get a key made for me?"

There were three more calls—customer calls. Nothing big and all-encompassing, but small was okay. Anything was better than thinking about Zac, kissing and keys.

Distractions, that's what she needed.

As if on cue, the bell jingled above the door. A blond girl walked in—no, that wasn't accurate, she breezed in with a huge smile on her face.

"Markie?" she asked.

"Yes, I'm Markie Walkowicz. Can I help you?" The girl didn't look like Markie's usual sort of client. She was about forty years too young.

"Oh, Markie, I knew it was you. You look just like your mother, except without the wrinkles. But just look at her and it's like a mirror twenty years into the future. Maybe even less. I mean, you work outside, and that means sun damage. You could have even more wrinkles than your mom."

Wrinkles? Thinking about wrinkles wasn't exactly the kind of distraction Markie had been wishing for. She pretended to smooth back her hair, but in actuality ran her fingers over her forehead, checking.

Oblivious, the girl sat down and without taking more than the merest breath, continued in a rush. "And it's not how you can help me, but how I can help you. Your mom says you're looking for a receptionist. Well, *here I am!* She said to tell you she scheduled a couple other interviews for this afternoon, but I'm sure you'll probably just want to cancel them. I'm here, I'm willing and I'm family."

"Family?" Markie asked, pretty sure she'd never seen this as yet unnamed girl before.

She was ready to ask the girl's name, when the girl said, "Let's see, my great-grandmother was married to your great-great-uncle Mark, who came over from Hungary in the early nineteen hundreds. It was 1905 to be exact. So, we're cousins of sorts, which is why your mom—I like to think of her as Aunt Estelle—suggested I come for an interview. Of course, I don't have any experience with this sort of thing—"

"You can use a computer though?" Markie asked.

"No, but I'm friendly. It's genetics, I guess. I mean, I met your mother just the other day while I was researching my family tree and she was just as friendly as friendly can be. And I think a friendly smile is better than knowing how to use a computer, don't you?"

"Do you have a resume?" Markie asked, not wanting to rate which was the more important skill for a receptionist, smiling or computer know-how.

Plus, she was pretty sure someone who told you that you were bound to be more wrinkly than your mother might not be classified as all that friendly despite the fact that she smiled a lot.

Really, anyone who was so smiley and bubbly was sort of suspicious.

"No. No resume. But we're cousins, what more do you need to know?" she asked, then continued to chatter away about her genealogy project.

Markie passed her a blank sheet of paper. "Why don't you leave your name and number and we'll get back to you. I should warn you that I wasn't actually planning to hire anyone till the spring."

"Oh, spring? I don't know if I'll be able to work here in the spring. I was planning to head to the shore. I like to spend the warm weather there."

"Make sure you take your sunblock. You wouldn't want to wrinkle," Markie muttered, not that her cousin noticed.

"I know, I know, you're broken up. Two cousins, working together, it would have been perfect…"

Markie was shaking her head as her cousin breezed back out of the office. She picked up the phone to call her mom, but set it back down when the door opened again and a young-ish man walked in. He smiled and said, "Miss Walkowicz? I'm Stanley Painter and I'm here to apply for the position."

Markie tried to smile her businesslike smile, but she wasn't up to interviewing another candidate and because of that she was pretty sure her smile was more of a grimace. It would probably giver her frown lines.

Stanley shook her hand, reached into his briefcase and withdrew a resume. He handed it to her. "I'm a student, working at finishing my degree and could really use a job. I'm proficient with computers and have a keen ability to organize. Your mother said you might be able to provide flexible hours to accommodate my schedule?"

Markie smiled. Now, this was more like it.

Way to go, Mom.

"That's possible, Stanley. What are you studying?"

"Well," he said, leaning closer, his voice a stage-whisper, "you don't have security clearance, so I won't go into detail, but since you'd be my boss, you have the right to know. I'm studying to be a spy."

Markie looked at the man across from her and had a hard time picturing him as a special agent.

"CIA?" she asked.

"CECS. Carlton Espionage Correspondence School."

Stanley forgot about security clearances as he began to tell her about his studies. By the time he left, Markie was sure she'd sprung more than a few new wrinkles. She dialed her mother's number.

"Hello?" her mother said.

"A cousin who would want the whole summer off so she could go to the shore, and a spy?" Markie asked without preamble.

"Oh, they came for the interviews. Who are you thinking of hiring?" her mom asked.

"Mom, I'd prefer root canal to employing either of them."

"Now, Markie—" her mother started as Markie's office door opened again.

"Got to go, Mom. Sorry, urgent business." She hung up and breathed a sigh of relief. Hurriedly, Markie gathered up her things. She wanted to get out of the office in case another candidate was on the way.

As she picked up her to-do list she saw that "make Zac a key" was on it.

Make him a key?

She was still fuming an hour later as she walked into the hardware store.

She wasn't sure she was happy about him staying with her, but she was even less happy at the thought of meeting the dead body again on her own.

But she was going to lay down the law. No kissing. No tenderly brushing hair off her cheek.

Oh, yeah, he probably thought she'd been too flustered to notice the hair thing, but she'd noticed and she wasn't putting up with any more of that.

And top on her list of requirements? Zac was definitely staying in the guest room.

She was going to set some rules. Zac could move in, but only until they found the body.

Zac Marshall was simply the lesser of two evils.

She thanked the hardware store man as she paid for the key and stepped back outside. She spotted Manning walking into Bartie's Books.

The big tattletale.

Fiery indignation flamed in her chest.

She was going to go give that bigmouth a piece of her mind.

Weren't cops supposed to be like priests or psychiatrists and keep your secrets to themselves?

Probably not.

But they should be.

She barreled into the store. Even the smell of new books, which normally comforted her, couldn't soothe her ire.

She spotted Manning at the counter waiting to get his purchases rung up.

"Hey, blabbermouth," she said by way of greeting.

Manning spotted her and his cheeks flushed a dark crimson.

Ha. He was embarrassed because he'd ratted her out. The fink.

Then she saw him move his books to the side of the counter.

"What do you want?" he asked, trying to sound tough as he distanced himself from the books.

She walked right in front of him and did a Port Richmond finger waggle. "You told your aunt that the body reappeared and then disappeared again."

"Maybe I happened to mention it." He shrugged. "So what?"

"So it's all over Port Richmond. Actually, it's probably all over Philly. I expect to hear it on the news tonight. But it can't be worse than my mom knowing. She's already called. I hate being hollered at on a Monday."

He gave the books another shove. "So, stop making these weird reports."

"I would if dead bodies stopped appearing at my house."

"Well—" he started to say just as Markie reached past him and grabbed the two books. "Hey!"

She looked at the cover. "Lori Foster and Catherine Mann. Good choices."

"I wouldn't know. My aunt asked me to pick them up."

"Your aunt reads mysteries," Markie commented.

"She reads a lot of things," Manning said with another shrug. Only his nonchalant shrug didn't quite match up with the slightly pink tinge in his cheeks.

"Ha! Bella doesn't read romance. She laughs at my mom and me because we're such fans."

"Figures you like romance," he said, trying to scoff, but it didn't come out any more convincing than his shrug had.

"From the looks of it, so do you."

"I ... I ..."

Bull's-eye.

Matt Manning, the tough cop extraordinaire, the tattle-tale patrolman, read romance. There was nothing wrong with that. As a matter of fact, if Manning wasn't on her least-liked list, she'd like that he was a man who recognized that love made the world go round.

But he was on the list, so she gave her figurative knife a small twist. "Why's a tough guy like you embarrassed to be caught reading romance?"

"Of course not. I mean, I'm not embarrassed because I don't read them. Listen, there's my radio. Got to go."

He ran from the store.

The clerk looked at the books in Markie's hand. "Want me to ring those up?"

She smiled. "Yes, I definitely do."

Oh, yeah. Manning was on her list. Spreading embarrassing stories about her all over town.

And once you were on a Walkowicz list…

Manning was about to learn how dangerous a position he was in.

Suddenly she had a plan for revenge.

Now if only she could figure out what to do with Zac and his place on her list… and in her house.

Waiting for Markie to open her front door, Zac had a feeling the evening was going to be difficult.

Well, not actually the evening, but rather the woman he'd be sharing the evening with.

But he had a plan.

As she opened the door, he leaned over and planted a big, sloppy brotherly kiss on Markie's cheek. "Hi, honey, I'm home. How was your day?"

He walked right past her into the house, dropped his bag on the floor, took off his coat and hung it neatly on one of the nearby wall hooks.

"Long. And it looks like it's not going to get any shorter because I don't see a pizza box in your hand. You said you were bringing pizza," she said in a growly sort of feed-me voice.

Markie wasn't one of those wimpy, eat-next-to-nothing women. She liked eating. And she got testy if she didn't eat regularly. He'd always liked that about her.

No worry about picking at food like a bird and Markie. She had curves...curves that looked pretty good in Zac's estimation.

"I didn't bring pizza. I did better." He shot her a smile, hoping to throw her off the fact that *his* better probably wasn't *her* better.

"Better than pizza?" She gave him a suspicious look, but at least she'd let him in and hadn't tossed his overnight bag out on the lawn.

He was making progress.

"Yes, better than pizza. We're supposed to be at my mom's for dinner at six."

Rather than smile—not that he'd been expecting a smile, but after all, a guy could only hope—she groaned. "Dinner at your mom's is not better than pizza."

"Are you saying that my mother can't cook?" he asked with mock indignation.

"No, I'm not saying that. As a matter of fact, your mom's a fantastic cook. It's just that—"

"It's just what?" he pressed.

"She knows I saw the body again. She has to know. That weasel Manning spilled the beans. It's okay, though. I've got a plan to get him back."

She smiled a wicked little smile.

This time it was Zac who groaned.

He almost felt sorry for Manning.

Almost, but not quite.

"Aren't you a little old for childish revenge? After all, it's been eleven months and you never got Joel back for walking out on you."

"I didn't need to get Joel back. After all, he's suffered. Suffered a great loss. No punishment I gave him could make it worse."

"What loss?" Zac asked.

She looked insulted. "Me. He lost me. He might not realize he's suffering yet, but he is. And someday he's going to realize he let the best thing in his life get away from him."

Zac couldn't deny the logic in that. He'd lost Markie eleven months ago as well, and suffering was the right word for it.

"So what's the plan for Manning?" he asked, knowing when a Walkowicz was out to get someone, nothing could save them.

"I'm not telling, but I'll make you a deal. I'll go to dinner at your mother's if you'll stop at the police station to pick up something you forgot."

The police station?

Her revenge was going to take place at the station?

Zac didn't like the sound of that.

She would be surrounded by cops when she exacted her retribution. He had to admit that, to date, he didn't think she'd ever tried any illegal revenge, but she was annoyed enough at Manning that he wouldn't put it past her.

"I didn't forget anything," he stated.

"Oh, I'm sure you can think of something you just can't live without until tomorrow."

"Swear to me that what you're planning is perfectly legal and won't permanently scar and injure Manning."

She chuckled a wicked little chuckle. "Do psychological scars count?"

Zac tried to look stern, but he smiled instead. "No."

"Then I can honestly swear it's legal and he won't be physically injured. If he's a real man, he won't even be psychologically injured ... at least not much."

"Fine," he said, his curiosity outweighing any sympathy he might feel for Manning. "We'll stop."

"Great. I'll get my purse."

Markie was smiling... it was the kind of smile that made Zac glad that Manning was higher on Markie's list than he was.

"You're sure it's not illegal?" he asked again. He'd hate to have to bail her out of jail.

"Positive," she promised.

Markie obviously forgot the eating-at-his-mother's part of the evening. She was silent, but practically radiated her excitement as they drove to the station.

He pulled up and parked, then she followed him into the front of the building humming a tuneless little happy song.

"Wait here," he said, giving her the evil eye of warning.

"Sure thing," she agreed happily.

He walked around the corner, waited half a second, then peeked back around.

Markie was talking to Harrington at the front desk. She reached in her purse and handed him something. Something that looked like a book.

Harrington laughed.

Zac didn't even pretend to go to the back and get something, he simply walked back up to Markie and Harrington.

"What's so funny?" he asked Harrington, trusting the cop to give him a straight answer more than he trusted Markie to give him one.

"Markie just returned something of Manning's. Something I'm sure he'll be happy to get back."

"I'm sure, too," Markie said in a bubbly little voice, her face alight with amusement. "I mean, there's nothing worse than starting a book and not getting to the last page."

"Yeah," Harrington said. "I'm sure he'll be relieved."

Markie was still humming as they walked back to his car. Zac finally figured out that the tune was supposed to be *Happy Days*.

Markie had never been able to carry a tune…she couldn't even grab it for a few notes.

"So now that it's done, tell me, just what did you do?" he asked. "I'm an accessory, after all."

She walked around to her side of the car and said, "I just returned Manning's property," then ducked inside.

"A book?" he asked as he settled in the driver's seat.

She nodded.

"How did you happen to come across Manning's book?" He started the car and backed out of the space, then headed toward his mother's.

"Well," she said, merrily, "there I was at the bookstore and there he was waiting in line to buy a couple books—"

"Books?"

"Romances. And we sort of got into it, so he left without buying them. Now I felt guilty, so I bought them for him, wrote his name in them so he won't feel obligated to return them to me, and dropped one off at the station."

"You said books," Zac said. "Plural. So, why not drop both off at the station?"

"I thought I'd stop at Bella's tomorrow and drop off the other one. That way, whichever place he goes to first, it'll be revenge city. And we both know how he likes spreading gossip at his aunt's."

"So, Manning reads romance and you let the world know?" he asked with a grin.

Markie nodded. "Sort of like I find dead bodies and he feels the need to let everyone know that."

"And you say I'm on the same list he is?" he asked. "What's my punishment going to be?"

"You've moved down the list a couple notches lately," she reluctantly admitted.

"So you believe I didn't chase Joel off?"

"Maybe."

He glanced over at her. She was looking out the window, rather than at him.

"So why didn't you return my calls?"

There was a long pause. "I didn't know what to say. I was embarrassed that you saw him for what he truly was...a snake. You know how I hate admitting I'm wrong. And—" she paused. "Well, there were lots of reasons I just didn't want to get into."

"All it would have taken was, 'Hi, Zac. I was wrong. I've missed you. Let's do dinner.'"

"Yeah, I thought about that," she admitted.

"So?"

"So what?"

"So why didn't you?"

"Well, I'm going to dinner with you now, aren't I?" Markie grumbled.

Some of Markie's happiness at planning Manning's downfall faded, mainly because she felt guilty.

She should have called Zac last week.

Heck, she should have called him sometime over the last eleven months.

He knew it and she knew it.

She couldn't blame Zac for pointing out a hard, but sad truth—Joel Summers was a jerk.

She hadn't asked herself why she was so mad at Zac all these months? Why she felt so uncomfortable at the thought of being with him?

Why, despite the fact she'd tried not to think of him, she'd thought of him often?

She hadn't asked herself in all these months, and she refused to ask herself now.

They rode in silence. Markie's bubble of happiness didn't just shrink; it popped.

The problem with having dinner at Zac's mom's was that she lived next door to Markie's mom.

And the last thing Markie wanted was for her family to find out she was eating with his family.

Markie was hoping she could sneak in and evade her mother.

"Hurry up," she urged Zac as she practically sprinted into his parents' house.

She felt rather smug when she reached Zac's living room without seeing her mother's curtains flutter.

"Markie, dear, it's been too long," his mother said, enveloping her in a hug.

"You just saw me last week," Markie reminded her. "But, thanks for letting me tag along for dinner."

"Honey, you know you're always welcome, especially now that you and Zac are living together."

Markie shot Zac an evil look and mentally revised her list. *Joel. The corpse. Zac. Manning. Mr. Zemjek and Sylvia Carson from high school.*

Yeah, Manning could move down now that he'd been partially paid back and Zac had to move up if he was telling his family they were cohabiting. Because if his family knew, then it was a sure thing her mother knew.

"We're *not* living together," Markie insisted, trying to do damage control. "Zac's just staying at the house because of the dead body. As soon as we find it, he's going home."

"If you say so," Mrs. Marshall said in a rather I-don't-believe-your-denial sort of way. "Come into the dining room, it's almost time to eat."

Markie noticed that the dining room table was set for eight. She did a quick head count. Zac. His mom. His dad. Herself.

Math wasn't her strongest subject, but she was pretty sure that was only four.

"Uh, Mrs. Marshall, are you expecting other people?"

Right on cue the doorbell rang, the front door flew open.

Markie's mom and dad walked in. "Markie! Oh, your father and I are so happy, aren't we, Stan?"

"Yes," her dad said, though he didn't look happy at all. He looked hungry. Markie noted it was about a half hour past his dinnertime.

Markie's whole family liked eating...and eating on time. Her stomach was rumbling.

"Is dinner ready?" her dad, getting right to the point, asked.

"Almost," Mrs. Marshall chirped.

"We'll stay here and turn on the game," Mr. Marshall suggested.

Her father seemed happy enough to join Mr. Marshall on the living room sofa. Zac followed and grabbed a chair.

He was deserting her. Leaving her to deal with her mom and his mom.

The rat.

"Why don't you ladies join me in the kitchen," Mrs. Marshall said to Markie and her mom. "We just have to wait for the girls. They're so excited."

Markie didn't have to ask who the girls were. Everyone who knew them referred to Mrs. Marshall's unmarried twin sisters as *the girls*.

Andrea and Erin would go to their graves as *the girls*.

"What are they excited about?" Markie asked.

"Why you and Zac, of course," Mrs. Marshall said as she stirred something in a bowl. It was sort of white; Markie couldn't tell what it was and knew her mother would consider it rude if she asked.

"Like we said the other day when we caught you at dinner," Mrs. Marshall continued, "we always knew you two were meant to be together."

"Ha!" Markie scoffed under her breath.

"What was that, dear?" her mother asked.

"I said, ha!" Markie said louder. "Zac and I aren't meant to be anything."

The men cheered at something on the television.

"I hate football," Mrs. Marshall muttered.

"So do I," Markie's mother said.

"Me, too," Markie agreed. "I can't live with a man who likes football. So don't get your hopes up about me and Zac. He'll be watching football at his house as soon as we find the body."

Her mother sighed. "If you'd been a teacher, there wouldn't be—"

"There'd still be a body, Mom."

The kitchen door banged against the wall and Markie groaned as *the girls* walked in and hugged her.

"We're so glad you're going to be part of the family. So, when's the wedding?" Andrea asked.

"Wedding?" Markie choked.

"Wedding?" Zac echoed from the doorway.

He was coming to her rescue. Markie decided maybe she'd let him live.

Maybe.

"Of course a wedding," Erin said. "Paula told us you were moving in with Markie."

"Yes, I moved in," he said with a grin.

Why on earth wasn't he protesting? Why wasn't he explaining the reason he'd moved in?

Markie shot him a look and then, to his aunts, she said, "Mrs. Marshall was wrong. He's not really moving in. Visiting. Guarding. Yes, he's guarding against dead bodies. He's my *bodyguard.*"

"Oh, no," Mrs. Marshall groaned. "Not again?"

"Yes. This morning," her mother said. "If she'd been a teacher she'd be married and have a witness."

"If she were a teacher and married, she couldn't marry my Zac."

Mrs. Marshall had made a point in her favor…at least Markie thought it was in her favor. She wasn't sure, so she didn't say anything about it.

"Okay, now that everyone's here, let's eat. I've got a nice pot roast. Why doesn't everyone sit down and—"

"Sorry. Zac and I just stopped in to tell you that we aren't going to be able to stay for dinner. He has an emergency."

"What sort of emergency?" her mother asked.

"It has to do…" Markie paused, "with the body. That's all we can say. Now we've got to go. Thanks so much for everything, Mrs. Marshall."

"Call me Mom," Zac's mother instructed.

Markie sprinted for the front door grabbing Zac's arm and pulling him with her.

"What about the game?" he muttered.

"Screw the game. Get me out of here."

"What about the wedding plans?" Andrea asked.

"Yes. I was thinking June," Erin added.

"June's a nice month," Zac, ever helpful, said.

"There are no wedding plans," Markie called to them.

"That's what we said about the body, but you insist there is one, so there must be a wedding too," her mother proclaimed.

Markie ignored her mother's logic and pushed Zac out the door toward the car.

"You're dead," she threatened.

"I don't think threatening a cop is very wise … especially one who didn't get his mother's world-famous pot roast."

"You made it sound like you were moving in with me on more than a short-term basis."

"I am. That's what the bag's all about. I'll bring more by later in the week."

"You're not moving in with me. You're visiting. Just a bodyguard."

"I know what body I'd like to guard, to watch, to touch, to—" He let the sentence trail off and just leered at her.

"Oh, come on, Zac. Didn't you use that same line on Dara Michaels in high school when we were playing basketball? *I want to guard Dara?* If I recall correctly, it didn't work then, and it definitely isn't working now."

"Can't blame a guy for trying," he said.

Zac Marshall had kissed her earlier, and now he'd leered at her and talked about touching her?

Markie might not have tons of experience with leers, but she knew one when she saw one. His eyes narrowed and his eyebrows rose.

Plus, he made a little frown. Not an I'm-annoyed sort of frown, rather just a crooked little twist of his lips that made her knees turn to jelly, her breathing get harder.

It made her want to kiss him.

Kiss Zac?

She was definitely losing her mind.

She'd let him kiss her earlier simply because he'd caught her off guard.

It wouldn't happen again.

She'd be more careful.

He might be staying with her, but she was going to keep her distance from Zac, his lips and his knee-weakening leers.

"Take me home," she demanded.

"Fine." He sounded almost jovial.

"And you better call and order a pizza. I'm starved."

"Let's turn around and get some roast then. My mom's roast beats pizza any day of the week."

"No way. I'm not going back in there and face not just my mom, but yours. Plus your aunts. Maybe if you'd been on my side—"

There was no teasing left in his tone as he interrupted and said, "I'm always on your side, Markie, whether you know it or not."

She couldn't think of anything to say to that, so she just said, "Anyway, you promised me pizza."

"Fine. But you're going to owe me ..." he said softly, letting the phrase hang there a second before adding, "for missing the pot roast."

He didn't sound angry at all. Instead, the soft gravelliness of his voice made a shiver slide down her spine and land squarely in the center of her body. Warm, tingly and full of images of paying back Zac.

Torturing him in ways she'd never imagined torturing him before.

"Are you thinking about how you're going to pay me back?" he asked.

"Just what do you think I owe you?"

"I'll think of something."

"Is that a threat or a promise?" she surprised herself by asking.

"Which would you prefer?" he countered.

"I'd prefer that things would get back to normal."

"Markie, there's nothing normal about you."

She wasn't quite sure if that was a compliment or not. She decided not to find out and practiced ignoring him the rest of the way home.

But as she watched him go in and retrieve their pizza, she realized ignoring Zac was getting harder and harder. Whatever it was they were developing was different than their friendship had been. She didn't want to analyze that difference, so she didn't.

She focused on the pizza aroma flooding the car and wouldn't allow her thoughts to stray beyond dinner.

She wouldn't allow herself to explore the new feelings that she was developing for Zac.

When they got home she took the box into the kitchen, took a couple slices on a plate, a can of soda and an entire box of Ho Hos.

"Make yourself at home," she said as she headed toward the stairs.

"What are you doing?" he asked.

"Going to my room and going to bed. Today's been stressful and I need my rest."

"You're not going to eat dinner with me?" He sounded disappointed.

Time to lay down the law. "Listen, you're here to protect me from dead bodies, not for eating together or kissing."

"Who mentioned kissing? I didn't mention kissing."

Damn.

"There's been kissing and there won't be any more," she stated.

"Why?" he asked.

She tried to think of some witty retort, but couldn't. So she simply settled for, "Because."

"That's not much of an answer."

It wasn't, but rather than agreeing with him, she said, "I don't owe you an answer."

"How about a Ho Ho?" he asked, eyeing the box.

"Not on your life." There just weren't enough Ho Hos in the house to share.

Let's face it, there wasn't enough of a house to share, at least not with Zac.

He was laughing as she stormed up the stairs with her supper, not to mention those Ho Hos.

8

Tuesday morning, Markie snuck out of the house long before Zac had to be up for work. She wasn't ready for the intimacy of sharing a morning with him.

It wasn't as if it were all that hard to get up before him. After all, she'd hardly slept. And every time she had managed to doze off, she dreamed.

No corpses this time, although after seeing it again, that's what she'd expected to dream about.

But no.

Her dreams were of Zac.

And instead of just thinking about kissing him, she *was* kissing him. Hard and long.

Talk about nightmares.

Markie was out of the house before six no problem at all.

She still checked out the window before going onto the front porch, but the coast was clear.

She had Manning's other book tucked in her bag, and a list of clients to visit today, starting with Mrs. Johns.

She wanted Markie to paint her kitchen.

Yellow.

Bright yellow.

The older lady's vision was failing. Markie figured she'd chosen the bright yellow so that she'd know what room she was in.

She taped off the trim and was actually humming as she started rolling on the paint. It might be bright, but it was cheery.

Markie felt her mood lighten as she worked.

It was going to be a good day. She could just feel it in her bones. The universe owed her a good day. Just one. And this was it.

This was—

She heard the kitchen door open.

"What do you think, Mrs. Johns?" Markie asked.

She looked up and saw... her mother walk in.

No, not walked.

Waltzed.

Her mother *waltzed* in and appeared ready for a fight.

Markie's mood darkened despite the bright wall.

"Marquette Ann Walkowicz, leaving dinner last night was just rude."

"Zac had an emergency at work. You know how tough it is to be a cop," she said.

That was her story and she was sticking to it.

Suddenly, she remembered they'd never finished discussing all the would-be receptionists her mother had sent.

Hoping to sidetrack her, Markie said, "By the way, when I asked you to draw up that job description, I didn't mean I was ready to hire anyone right now."

"Oh. I did tell a few other people to stop in, but I won't tell anyone else."

"Thanks," Markie muttered. "Can you call them back and cancel?" she asked, not feeling overly hopeful.

"That would be rude. Now, about last night. Even ruder," her mother folded her arms across her ampleish chest as a form of punctuation, "even ruder than leaving was not telling me you were moving in with a man. Can you imagine how I felt having his parents know before me?"

Markie should have known her mother was unsidetrackable.

"Actually I didn't move in with a man, the man moved in with me…into the guest room. Separate bedrooms, Mom. There's nothing between us but a bedroom wall and a dead body."

She leaned over and coated the roller with more paint, then slid it across another swatch of wall.

Yes, all she and Zac had was a body and a bedroom wall between them.

And a kiss. A heck of a kiss. And maybe a few fantasies. And dreams. Hot dreams. And a history.

Yes, that was absolutely all there was between her and Zac.

"He's just there until we find out what's happening with the body," she assured her mother.

Her mom didn't look assured as she said, "You and Zac living together—"

Markie interrupted and reminded her mother, "Separate bedrooms. We're in separate bedrooms."

"That will change soon enough," her mother warned. "I've seen you two together, watched you both grow up for goodness' sake. You might start out in separate bedrooms, but it's only a matter of time until you're sharing one. I think the girls were right; June is the perfect time for a wedding."

"There's not going to be a wedding ever again. Been there. Done that. Wouldn't recommend it to anyone."

"You didn't actually get a whole wedding, just a start. A false start, at that. Joel doesn't count," her mother assured her.

"Why?"

"He was an ass."

"Mother," she gasped when she was able to get enough breath into her lungs to speak.

To the best of her knowledge, her mother had never used a swear word. Not that ass was much of a swear word, but for her mother, it was the equivalent of something much stronger.

"Don't *Mother* me. I meant what I said. Joel Summers was an ass to leave you at the altar saying he needed to find himself. Found himself with the stripper from his stag is more like it." Her mom gave a small snort of disgust. "Zac's not like that. He'd never let you down."

Markie hated to admit it, but her mother had a point. Look at the way Zac had come to help her, even though she'd pretty much shut him out of her life for eleven months. There was no hesitation on his part. She needed him and he was there.

"You're right. Zac's not like Joel. But still, I'm not marrying him. I'm not really even living with him." She stopped a moment then added, "But I think we're friends again."

The words felt right. Zac had always been her friend. Unfortunately, she'd been too stubborn to admit it.

"Do you want the wedding at St. Adalbert's again, or would that carry too many bad memories?" her mother asked, as if she hadn't heard a word Markie said. "It would be more convenient to use, since not only do we belong to the parish, but so does Zac's family. But I wouldn't want to if you think it's bad luck. I'm sure your father would understand."

"There's no question of luck … I'm not marrying Zac."

"Well, you can't live together in mortal sin."

"There's no sinning, mortal or venial. Separate bedrooms, Mom. We're in separate bedrooms."

"Markie, I wasn't born yesterday. And I have to say, I'm so glad he's at least half-Polish. Even though his father might not have been born Polish, having lived in the neighborhood so many years he almost counts as—"

Markie couldn't do this. She didn't want to have this conversation with her mother, so she interrupted and said the first thing she could think of... the one thing that might distract her single-minded mother from talk of mortal sins, wedding locations and Zac's heritage.

"Danny's not gay. You can stop looking for a boyfriend for him."."

It took her a moment to realize that she'd really said the words out loud.

She wasn't proud of them. Not proud at all. But it wasn't even lunch, and her mother was grilling her about getting married. Zac was sleeping in her guest room and she kept stumbling over bodies.

Sometimes a girl had to do what a girl had to do.

And in this instance, it worked. Her mother stood speechless a moment and then said, "What?"

"Danny's not gay. He's been seeing someone. A female someone. A secret someone."

"And?" her mother prompted.

"She's a good Polish girl. A little older, but nothing staggering."

"How much older?" her mother asked, her eyes narrowing. "Are we talking cradle robbing or simply a woman with taste?"

"Definitely not cradle robbing. Four years, give or take."

"Four years is nothing." Her mother paused a moment as she digested the information, then added, "Four years? Why, she's still plenty young enough to give me grandchildren. Of course, I want Danny to be happy, but I want grandchildren, too. Who is she?"

Markie might give up Danny, but she wasn't going to give up Babs.

Sacrificing a brother was understandable—a sisterly duty, even—but a good friend? No, she couldn't do that.

"I can't say. I was sworn to secrecy. But you'd approve."

Her mother's arms uncrossed and she smiled. "I think I'm going over to Danny's for lunch."

"Sounds like a plan," Markie said, feeling a stab of guilt. "Want to work this afternoon?"

"Sure." Her mother looked practically bubbly.

Estelle Walkowicz rarely bubbled.

She lectured.

She shot *looks*.

But she didn't bubble.

Markie smiled. "I've got a long list of appointments today."

"I know, I checked your appointment book…that's how I found you. And I found paperwork on a cell phone. Why do you need a cell phone?"

Markie didn't want to admit that she'd picked it up yesterday so that next time she found the body, she wouldn't have to go find a phone. So she said, "I needed one for work."

"I guess that makes sense," her mother said, nodding her head in approval. "I'll call you later. And thanks for letting me know about Danny."

"No problem." Okay, no problem for her, but her brother Danny might just do her in after this. "I've got to run."

"Where are you heading next?"

Markie smiled. "I've got some icicles to knock down and a squeaky floor to de-squeak, then I have to drop something off at Bella's."

"Oh, and I didn't forget about you and Zac," her mom said, but there was no arm-crossing or eye-narrowing. She was still too happy about Danny possibly giving her grandchildren someday.

"I didn't figure you had," Markie said. She leaned over and kissed her mother's cheek.

Her mother gave her a quick buss back. "I love you," she said.

"I love you, too, Mom."

Ahhh.

"I'll talk to you about things later," her mom called cheerily as she walked out Mrs. Johns's kitchen door.

Markie went back to painting, though the yellow didn't seem quite as cheery. She tried to ignore the wedding bells in her head that her mother was trying to ring.

Markie preferred to think of them as the chimes of her impending doom. Because she was sure their talk later would start right back up with mortal sins and churches.

All she'd done by giving up Danny was buy some time.

She was going to take care of Mrs. Johns's kitchen, then on to Mrs. Sanchez's.

She thought about the book safely tucked in her bag and her mood lightened again.

Then she'd pay a small visit to Bella's.

"I'm going to kill your girlfriend," Manning growled.

Zac was sitting at his desk making the motions of going over some files. Actually, he was fuming because Markie hadn't just hidden in her room last night, ruining all his hopes for a pizza seduction.

No, she'd snuck out this morning before he got up.

The coward.

Now he had to deal with her little practical joke?

He felt his mood slip a little lower. In fact, he felt dangerously close to rock-bottom.

"I don't have a girlfriend, but I'm assuming you're talking about Markie."

"You're living with her, right?"

"Just until we find out what's going on. We're not living together as in *living together*, if that's what you're asking. Not that it's any of your business," he added.

And not that he wasn't going to do his best to change that as soon as possible.

"I can tell you what's going on. She's nuts. Crazy. Insane. And she's also dead when I get my hands on her." Manning's face was an interesting shade of pink.

Zac's mood lightened slightly. "You know, I don't think it's very smart to threaten to kill someone."

"Figuratively kill her," Manning said through gritted teeth. "Not literally."

"What did she do?" Zac asked.

"Left this for me at the front desk," he said, tossing a book on the desk.

Zac picked it up, made a show of reading the back cover. "It looks good. I'd say she did you a favor."

"Tell her to save her favors. She did it just to embarrass me."

"Really?" Zac asked, setting the book back down and sliding it toward Manning.

"This was on the bulletin board," Manning said. He handed Zac a mock book cover someone had made on the computer. There was a woman staring adoringly at a taped-in photo of Manning.

Love Patrol was the title.

"Cute, huh?" Manning said. "And that's just the start. It seems my new nickname's Romeo. I'll never live it down. It's all Markie's fault."

"So you think sharing information—private information—about you with your peers and neighbors is less than helpful?"

"I…" Manning got the point. Zac could practically see it hit the young patrolman's thick skull. "Okay, I get it. Call her off."

"I will, but it might be too late for phase two," Zac said.

"There's more?" Manning asked, all the growl gone from his voice. He sounded nervous.

"Never piss a Walkowicz off. They're dangerous and devious."

"Hey, Marshall," Lt. Jan Wang hollered.

"Yeah?" he called back, ignoring Manning's exasperation.

"Wasn't that body your girlfriend found supposed to be wearing a plaid suit?"

"Yes," Zac stood. "Green and orange."

He'd dropped the swatch of the material off with a buddy at the lab, but there hadn't been anything particularly helpful about it. Basically, other than backing up Markie's story, it was a pretty useless piece of evidence.

"Uh, you might want to head over to Manchester Retirement Home," Wang said.

"Why?"

"Seems they found a 5292 in a gazebo out back, a Maury Desanti." She paused a moment, then added, "He's wearing a plaid suit."

Zac was out from behind the desk and heading for the door. "I'm on my way."

"Mind some company?" Manning asked.

He stopped and looked at Markie's nemesis. "You want to help?"

"Let's just say, I think I want to see if I owe your girl-friend an apology."

Zac nodded. "Come on."

❧ ❧ ❧

"You Told."

Markie groaned and wished she hadn't picked up the phone.

It had been a semigood afternoon.

She'd dropped the book off at Bella's, exacting the second part of her revenge, and come home to a quiet, bodyless house.

Markie had felt a bit of a pang that Zac wasn't home yet. It wasn't that she missed him or anything, she assured herself. It was simply that she was worried about the body turning up and not having a witness.

At this point, she'd even settle for her mother's hypothetical grandchildren.

She just knew that if she saw the body again and no one else did, she was going to make an appointment with a good psychiatrist.

Even she was beginning to doubt her own sanity, despite having found the small swatch of cloth.

And it wasn't just finding a dead body that had her doubting her mental health; it was the fantasies about Zac that she couldn't quite hold at bay.

That she wasn't sure she wanted to hold at bay anymore.

And that was just crazy.

Her and Zac?

They were friends, not lovers. But maybe it wasn't so insane thinking that maybe they could be.

Images started to unfold in her mind.

She smiled.

"Markie? Are you there?"

Her smiled turned to a frown as she pulled herself back from pleasant fantasies to an unpleasant reality.

Danny on the phone.

"Yeah, I'm here," she said.

"How could you tell Mom I was dating?" he asked. She could hear the post-Mom-interrogation frustration in his voice.

"Actually, what I told her was that you weren't gay."

"What?" Danny asked with total indignation.

"She worried that you were gay because you hadn't dated in a while," Markie explained. "She wouldn't have minded your being gay. She was looking for a guy to fix you up with," she felt obliged to assure her brother. "It's just that she'd have been hurt if you felt you couldn't go to her. Anyway, I told her you weren't gay to make her feel better."

"Yeah," Danny said, skepticism in his voice. "And of course it had nothing to do with getting her off your back about the mysterious disappearing dead body, right?"

"Of course not. What sort of sister do you think I am?" She tried to sound indignant, but didn't think she'd quite managed it.

"I think you're a scheming sort of sister who just gave up *my* love life in order to get Mom off *your* back."

"Listen, I didn't give her any specifics. I didn't say it was Babs. I just..." She couldn't think of any other good arguments for telling on Danny. "Well, I didn't say it was Babs."

"There's nothing to tell about me and Babs anyway." His voice had a sound of finality to it. "It's over."

Markie should mind her own business. She might have told her mother that Danny wasn't gay, but she didn't go around butting into her brother's business.

His relationship with Babs was between the two of them.

Now, her mother wouldn't think twice about butting in, about offering unneeded and unasked-for advice.

But she wasn't like her mother.

She minded her own business.

Why, look at everything going on in her life. She didn't need to try to help Danny and Babs. Why, she couldn't even help herself.

She was going to stay out of it.

She was going—

She heard herself ask, "Since when are you the type of guy who quits?"

Why had she done that?

"Since it's hopeless," Danny said. "All Babs sees is the age difference."

Okay, that was it. She was done butting in. He'd said it was hopeless.

She was going to just leave it alone and mind her own business.

Say goodbye, Markie, she instructed herself.

"What do you see?" she asked instead.

"What do I see?" Danny repeated. "I see the woman I love."

Oh, no, an admission.

She had to stop.

But she heard the pain in Danny's voice.

She'd witnessed Babs's pain the other day.

Instead of stopping, she simply dove in and said, "So don't give up. Remember when you got lost at the Smithsonian? You were so little, but you didn't freak out. You calmly found a security guard and made him help you find us. You're the type of person who sees a problem and fixes it. That's how you are. You fix things. Fix this."

"I can't make myself age almost five years overnight," he said.

"No. You can't." Knowing that she was treading very close to giving up information on a friend, a definite no-no in the best friend rule book, she said, "I don't think that the age difference is the real problem."

"I don't have a clue what else it could be. We're perfect for each other."

"Maybe that's it. After years of dating the wrong men, maybe dating the right one is scary. Maybe Babs is afraid she'll mess it up with you. Maybe it's just easier to push you away."

Okay, so she didn't quite give Babs up. She'd said *maybe* after all.

"You think?" he asked, a bit of hope filling his voice.

"Maybe," she said again, just to make sure he knew she wasn't giving up a friend's confidence.

"So what do I do?"

"You'll think of something. But giving up isn't an option. You owe it to yourself to see where this might lead." She paused a moment and added, "Sorry I told Mom you weren't gay."

"No harm. I guess having her hound me about my mystery woman is better than her deciding to fix me up on blind dates with other guys."

Markie smiled at the thought. "Yeah, there's that."

A beep signaled that Markie had another call.

"Listen, there's someone on the other line. Let's meet at the park...you know where, and see what we can come up with."

When they were younger, their group of friends had claimed a big rock in the middle of a small stand of trees at the park as their own. It had been years since she'd been there, but matters like this required someplace special.

"Great. I'll call you."

Danny owed it to himself to see where he and Babs might go. Didn't Markie owe as much to herself? Should she see just where this attraction to Zac could lead?

As the question beat around in her head, she clicked her flash button and picked up the other line.

"Markie?"

Her heart did this odd little flutter.

Zac.

"Yes?" she asked, sounding breathless to her own ears.

She forced herself to put more force in her voice and said, "What's up?"

"Listen, I'd like you to come over to Manchester Retirement Community."

Someone in the background shouted, "5292."

"Why? What happened?"

"I think I found your body."

9

"I don't understand," Markie murmured again.

When she arrived, Zac had led her back to the frozen garden behind the retirement community.

A frozen garden with a gazebo in its center.

A gazebo that contained a rather frozen corpse wearing a plaid suit.

"Come on," Zac said, trying to lead her away from the body.

He'd been pretty sure this was Markie's corpse and now she'd confirmed it.

Rather than answering questions, locating the body just left him with more.

"It's him," she said. "I know it's him. But I don't understand. How did he get from my front porch, to my backyard, to here? It's at least a fifteen-minute drive from my house to the home. He didn't walk."

"Come on, honey." Zac took her elbow and led her down the path and out of the garden. "The coroner says he can't see any signs of foul play. We'll know more in a couple days, after the autopsy."

"But that doesn't make sense either. If there was no foul play, then why didn't someone just call for help when he died?"

"I don't know," Zac said. "I checked his suit, there's a piece torn off the jacket."

"Our fabric swatch," she murmured.

"Yeah."

Markie looked cold. He reached out and zipped the zipper of her coat.

She didn't push him away. It wasn't exactly a heartening sign. After all, she'd had a shock. But Zac decided to press his luck and put his arms around her and pull her close.

She didn't pull away.

As a matter of fact, she snuggled closer.

Something twisted in his chest. There was desire there, but there was something more as well.

There had always been something more where Markie was concerned.

"Do you know who it is?" she asked, her voice slightly muffled by his jacket.

"His name's Desanti. According to the staff, no one's seen him since the weekend before last."

She pulled back so she could look at him. "That fits with the first time I tripped over him. Did they report him missing to the police?"

"No. This is a senior citizen complex, more apartments than an actual care facility. The residents are free to come and go as they please, and Mr. Desanti was reputed to be a ladies' man. He was gone overnight frequently. No one thought anything of it."

"It just doesn't make sense." She put her head back against his chest.

Feeling emboldened by what she'd already allowed, he reached out and stroked her hair. It was in a casual, messy sort of ponytail.

Markie had never been the kind of woman to spend hours primping. She didn't need any enhancements. She was what she was, and that had always been more than enough for him.

"I know it doesn't make sense," he said, his hand toying with the end of the ponytail. "But there's nothing more we can do, at least not until after the autopsy."

"So now what?" she asked.

"Let's go home."

Zac insisted on driving her home. One of his buddies followed with his car.

Markie was glad. She felt out of sorts. Disconnected. Confused.

He let them both into the house and said, "I'm ordering Chinese."

"Okay," she said, tossing aside her jacket and curling up on the couch. She pulled the afghan over her. She just couldn't seem to get warm.

"Do you want anything special?"

"No." She didn't want anything except answers.

Zac busied himself around the apartment, called for the takeout, started a fire and made a few calls in the kitchen.

She could hear the murmur of his voice. It was comforting. The dips and peaks of it.

She laid her head back against the cushion and closed her eyes. She tried to wrap her brain around poor Mr. Desanti turning up at the nursing home. She tried to come up with some logical explanation how he got from here to there, but she couldn't.

This entire situation defied logic.

The doorbell rang.

"I'll get it," Zac said.

"No, maybe they'll go away," she said, but he'd already opened the door.

"Where is she?"

Oh, yeah, this was just what she needed.

"In the living room," Zac the traitor said.

Her mother.

The Port Richmond grapevine was at work again.

"Markie, honey," her mother cried as she ran across the living room and enveloped Markie in a hug. "I heard."

"What did you hear?"

Her mother sat next to her on the couch. "I heard that they found your body."

"How…"

"Well, Bella heard that there were police cars and an ambulance at Manchester Home. She does a Mrs. Warren's hair on Tuesdays. Mrs. Warren lives there and she was talking about someone being found dead in the gazebo. So Bella called her nephew for an update. She's a bit miffed. He wasn't nearly as forthcoming as he usually is. She practically had to pull the information out of him. Finally, he said they found your body frozen solid. It wasn't just your imagination. I said this is one of the coldest winters on record—"

"Bella," Markie prompted, trying to get her mother back on track.

"Oh, so Bella of course wanted to know who was dead. Her nephew had to leave before they made an ID."

"Of course she wants to know," Markie muttered. Bella, the hub of Port Richmond gossip—heck, probably the hub for all gossip in the entire Philadelphia metropolitan area— needed all the facts.

"By the way, her nephew said he felt bad for doubting you."

"I'll just bet he does," Markie said. But whether or not he felt bad, whether or not she'd exacted a bit of revenge, Manning was still on her list.

"Of course, when Bella mentioned you left his book at the salon, she said he would have to make it up to you."

Markie was sure Manning would at least try.

"Anyway, Matt said it had to be your body. After all, how many dead men could be wearing plaid suits in the Philadelphia area? So Bella called me, and here I am. I came to comfort you."

"I don't need to be comforted," Markie assured her mother. "His name was Desanti."

Her mom didn't seem all that concerned with finding out the name for Bella. She just hugged Markie again and said, "Every girl needs her mother when she's found a body."

Markie didn't point out that she hadn't found the body today. Yesterday maybe and last week, maybe, but not today. She'd simply identified it today.

She shivered as she remembered. "I'm fine, Mom."

"Really?" Her mom looked skeptical.

"Zac's taking care of me."

"Oh." She paused. "Oh. Well, then, I'd better go. I'm sure there are a bunch of messages on my machine. People who thought you were crazy and now have to eat crow."

Her mother stood up, paused a moment, then leaned down and gave Markie another kiss. "I'm sorry I doubted you. You don't have to be a teacher if you don't want to."

Markie laughed. "Thanks, Mom."

"And honey?"

"Yes?"

"I love you."

And with that, her mother, the whirlwind, blew out of the house, leaving Markie and Zac alone.

"So, everything's okay with your mom?" Zac asked, slinking back into the living room when her mother left.

"Coward," Markie teased.

"Hey, Estelle Walkowicz is scary under normal situations. Hiding in the kitchen isn't cowardly, it's smart. I was listening for the doorbell though. The food's on its way. Hungry?"

It was an innocent enough question. But as Markie studied Zac, she realized she was hungry, and it had nothing to do with Chinese food. It had everything to do with the man standing in front of her.

When he'd wrapped her in his arms this afternoon, she knew the embers of desire that had been sizzling just under the surface were growing. She wasn't sure how much longer she could keep them banked.

She wasn't even sure she wanted to.

The phone rang.

Saved by the bell.

"Maybe I'd better get that," Markie said, welcoming an excuse to give herself some distance from Zac.

Truth was, she didn't want a break. She wanted to take his hand, lead him to her room and have her way with him. It would be a long, hot sweaty way.

But…but this was Zac. Zac her buddy. Heck, Zac her enemy. Her protector, her aggravation, her…any number of things, but not her lover. Not that she wasn't attracted to Zac. A woman would have to be blind and deaf…and not very bright, not to be. But…

Back to the *but*. *But* this was Zac.

"Are you going to get that?" he asked.

"Yeah." She picked up the phone. "Hello?"

"Are you okay?" It was Danny.

Danny to the rescue.

"Yeah, I'm fine."

"I heard they found your body."

"Looks like."

"How did he die? Who was he?"

"Desanti…" she said. "He lives…he *lived* at Manchester Retirement Home. They don't know how he died yet."

"But you're fine?" Danny asked again.

She glanced at Zac, who was setting the dining room table, and her heart rate sped up.

Palpitations.

She was having palpitations.

But she didn't share that with Danny. She just said, "Yes, I'm fine. Thanks for worrying."

"Anytime. I'll call tomorrow."

Zac came back out of the kitchen with two steaming cups.

She knew they contained tea.

She knew so many things about Zac.

Including the fact that he was making her heart race at an unnatural speed. She wanted him.

She just wasn't sure what to do about her desire. How to act on it without losing his friendship. She'd missed him so much over the last eleven months, she didn't want to risk losing him again.

Zac set up for dinner as Markie finished her phone conversation.

Markie was stubborn.

She got something in her head and she just couldn't shake it out.

That's why she was still holding him at arm's length, even though she'd confessed she didn't believe he'd chased Joel off.

If he waited for her to come to her senses and realize there was something between them, friendship at the very least, but possibly more…she'd never admit it.

So Zac was going to have to give her a push.

It's how he taught her to ride that bike.

No self-respecting six-year-old should still be using training wheels. He might have been only eight at the time, but he knew that much.

So, he'd borrowed his father's wrench, took off her training wheels and pushed her down the nearest hill.

Of course, he hadn't taken into account the fact that there was a street halfway down the hill, or that he'd neglected to make sure she knew how to brake.

He'd about died when she whizzed right out into the intersection and kept going full throttle down the hill.

Full throttle.

That's how Markie did everything.

Look at how she'd taken her business from her home to an office in less than a year.

Full throttle.

But she sometimes needed that push to get started.

He'd pushed her into the neighborhood pool to teach her to swim.

She'd gone from landlocked to fish in one afternoon.

He was friend enough to push her again.

He should have pushed her harder last year. He'd planned to when he went to her the night before her wedding.

But things didn't go as planned... the night ran on like some very bad play where a childhood friend realizes he's really in love with the girl, but too late—the girl is in love with someone else.

He'd gone to Markie the night before her wedding, urging her to call it off, but as she'd gone on and on about her feelings for Joel, he realized telling her he cared for her as more than a friend would be selfish, so he'd let it go.

She loved Joel.

He had to face the truth.

She was going to marry Joel Summers.

When Joel hadn't shown up at the wedding and Markie found out he'd run off with another woman, she'd accused him of knowing that Joel was cheating and had blamed him for not telling her that night.

He'd denied it. But when she pushed to know why he had wanted her to call the wedding off, he hadn't been able to offer a good explanation.

So she blamed him.

He figured he'd tell her eventually, but the words wouldn't come.

Not that he had much of a chance to let them come. He'd hoped she'd get over being mad eventually...she always did. But she hadn't...and, he was realizing now, he hadn't either.

It was time to come clean—past time—to tell her everything. And then...?

He'd have to see.

10

"Damn that Manning," Markie muttered as she stomped heavily into the house the next night.

Zac had spent the day on pins and needles. Anticipation warred with ... fear. He could chase a felon down the street, but he had a gut-deep fear that Markie would reject what he so wanted to offer.

But she was here now and watching her unlace her work-boots, he couldn't help but smile.

"What did Manning do now?" he asked, as she stripped off her coat and kicked off her boots, still muttering the whole time.

He could make out the occasional word like *Manning, damn, ticket, dork.*

"What did he do?" she repeated. "He's thrown down the gauntlet. *This* is war."

Zac shook his head. Whatever Manning had done wasn't wise. Wasn't wise at all. "I thought he started the war by telling everyone about your disappearing body."

"That was just an opening feint. He was just drawing me in. But this? Today? This was an all-out battle cry."

Zac waited, knowing she was just catching her breath.

"He wrote me a ticket. I was at St. Adalbert's helping Father with a light that kept shorting out, when that sneak

Manning left a parking ticket on my car. Said I was too close to the hydrant."

"Were you?" Zac asked, trying not to smile. After all, he didn't want to get on Markie's list tonight. What he wanted was her.

"Maybe I was technically too close," she practically mumbled, but picked up volume as she added, "but I wasn't blocking it. But that's not why he left it. It was an act of revenge."

"He might not have even known it was your car," Zac said.

"Oh, he knew all right. There was a little smiley face on the ticket by his name. He knew it was me. And truly, I was on God's business, working at the church and all. You'd think even a blabbermouth like Manning wouldn't risk God's wrath by ticketing me."

"To be honest, I'd be more worried about your wrath … it's a fearsome thing."

That made Markie smile, which had been his intent.

"Want me to get him assigned to crossing guard duty?" he asked.

She shook her head. "It's nice of you to offer, but I fight my own battles."

"Speaking of fighting … are we still fighting?"

"We're not fighting," she said, looking confused.

"You're sure? I mean, I know I was on your list for a long time. And want to be sure I'm totally off it now. We've called a truce."

"I admitted that I was wrong." She paused a moment and then added, "You didn't ever belong on the list."

"So, if we're no longer enemies, and I'm off the list, just what are we now, Markie?"

"Friends," she said, trying to sound certain. "I needed to blame someone when Joel left. You were convenient. I'm sorry for that."

"So, it's a truce. Want to make it official? We'll kiss and make up?"

She didn't look overly enthused at the suggestion.

"My apology isn't enough?" she asked.

"I don't know," he said thoughtfully. "Eleven months is an awful long time to be without a friend. That deserves at least a small kiss to make up."

"Fine." She put a small peck on his cheek.

"Wow, that was pitiful." He shook his head sadly. "Simply pitiful."

"Pitiful?" she asked, her cheeks flushing.

"Yep. That was absolutely the most pitiful kiss I've ever received. And you remember Laura Marie from school? Now she gave a pitiful kiss, though it wasn't her fault. I mean, not only braces but that horrible gear that wrapped around her head? Yeah, she had an excuse for bad kissing."

He shook his head and just stared at Markie sadly, holding back a grin.

He thought he'd wait. Wine her, dine her, then make his move. But he couldn't wait. He'd thrown down the gauntlet—her second challenge of the day—and if he knew Markie, she wouldn't be able to resist the challenge any more than she could let Manning's ticket go by.

"How about this?" She quickly gave him a small buss on the lips. Quick, chaste and over far too soon. "Better?"

"Maybe not as pitiful, but certainly not impressive."

"Like you could do better," she scoffed.

Ah, the invitation he'd been waiting for.

"I think I can manage better than that. To be honest, it won't be much of a challenge."

Before she could protest, he planted one on her lips.

Hard, probing.

He fed all his pent-up desires, all the frustration of being so close, but never close enough, all of it into that kiss.

She didn't protest. As a matter of fact, she actively joined in, deepening the kiss, wrapping her arms around his neck.

He pulled back and looked at her.

Her eyes were a little glassy and her breath was definitely ragged.

Then again, so was his.

"That wasn't exactly a kiss of making up," she murmured.

"It wasn't meant to be." He reached out and ran a finger lightly down her cheek, wrapped it round and trailed it along her jawline.

"Then what…" Markie started to ask what it was, but even to her ears the question sounded stupid.

She could see in Zac's eyes exactly what that kiss had been.

It was a kiss of seduction.

He wanted her.

And Markie could probably deal with his desire in a polite, but firmly declining manner, except for one *small* problem.

No, make that one big problem.

A big, growing, huge problem.

She wanted him, too.

If they took this relationship further, she could lose his friendship, a friendship she'd just gotten back.

She didn't think she was strong enough to lose it again.

"Markie." Zac's voice was a light breeze against her cheek, he was standing so close.

"You're my friend, Zac. I don't want to lose that. I might if we—"

"Made love?" he supplied.

She couldn't bring herself to say the words, so she simply nodded.

"Don't you get it yet? You never lost me. You couldn't lose me. I'm a part of you, just like you're a part of me. And I'm not talking about a lifetime of friendship, although that's part of it. I'm talking about this…about this spark that's always been there. It's more than a spark of awareness now. It's a full-fledged fire. And there's only one thing that will put it out."

Markie knew she'd lost the battle with herself—although it had been a rather sad battle at best.

She wanted this too much to say no.

And she realized with sudden clarity that the desire wasn't recent. Zac was right, it had always been there, a small spark in the corner of her awareness. She'd ignored it then, but couldn't any longer. It was too big, too hot.

Whether desire mixed with friendship was enough to sustain something more than one night was a question she'd answer later…tomorrow.

Right now, all she could think about was Zac.

"What if we don't want to put the fire out? What if I ask you to help it blaze."

She took his hand and led him to her room.

Zac looked at the woman sleeping so peacefully in his arms.

He'd wanted this for so long. And now that he had her, he knew that he'd never be able to let her go again.

Somehow he was going to have to convince her that they were meant for more than a friendship…that they were meant for something deeper and much more meaningful.

They were meant for love.

Somehow, he'd show her. This was a start, but he wasn't sure she saw the true implications. He'd tell her, show her.

But it would have to wait, he thought as he slipped into a deep sleep.

He awoke with a start, sure that he'd barely closed his eyes.

He looked around, not the least bit disoriented. He knew where he was…right where he belonged. Next to Markie Walkowicz.

He did look to see what had jarred him from his sleep.

The doorbell was ringing.

Markie's room was at the front of the house, her window looking down over the porch.

"Marquette Ann Walkowicz, I know you're in there," Markie's mom bellowed.

"You, too, Zachary Paul Marshall," came a second voice. His mother's voice.

The voices of doom.

He glanced at the clock.

Seven.

It had to be 7:00 p.m., not a.m.

Seven at night.

What would bring their mothers here at seven at night?

Markie sat up, gave him a quick kiss and said, "Do you suppose they'd go away if we just stayed inhere?"

"It's a nice thought, but no. Our moms are much too persistent for that."

She heaved a sigh. "I should have parked around the corner."

"Me, too."

"Hindsight is twenty-twenty."

She gave him an odd look and he wondered if she was having some brief glimpse of hindsight about what they'd done. Wishing they hadn't, or wishing they'd made love sooner?

He couldn't tell from her expression and he couldn't bring himself to ask.

"I'll go let them in. I'm betting I can dress faster than you can."

She smiled. "Thanks. And pick up your shoes on the stairs. I don't want any questions."

Did she plan to hide this new facet of their relationship from their families? Did she think this was just a one-time act?

If so, Zac would have to educate her on the true way of things when they ditched their moms.

Now that he had her, she wasn't going to slip away from him again.

"I'll get them," he said as he hurriedly tossed on his clothes and went to confront the guests, leaving Markie a few minutes to herself.

She tiptoed across the hall into the bathroom. She could hear the murmur of voices from downstairs.

She looked at her rather bedraggled self, and sighed as she tried to tame her bed head and then put on a bit of makeup, not for their uninvited company but for Zac. She wanted to look good for him.

And putting on makeup also gave her an extra minute to compose herself.

She'd made love to Zac.

She smiled and felt a bit flushed.

She decided to forgo the blush. She didn't need it.

Just thinking of what she'd done with Zac added a nice pinkness to her cheeks.

Oh, had they made love.

What would this mean to their relationship? She wasn't sure, but she didn't want to think about that. Didn't want to dull her happiness by worrying about it. She simply wanted to revel in the moment.

She'd made love to Zac.

She took a last look and hurried downstairs to join him. They needed to present a united front to whatever their mothers were up to now.

Her eyes found his as she walked into the room, forgetting all about mothers for just a moment.

He looked up as if he sensed her presence and smiled at her. A small, intimate smile that spoke volumes and left her knees strangely weak.

Markie forced herself to take in the rest of the room.

"Mom, Dad. Mrs. Marshall." She paused as she took in the two mystery guests. "Babs? Danny?"

"We stopped in to invite you both out for a late dinner. Paula rode with us because Zac's father's meeting us at the restaurant, along with half the neighborhood."

"What's going on?" Markie asked.

"This," Babs said, waggling her finger. "I left you a message today, but I guess you didn't get it."

Checking the answering machine hadn't been high on her list of things to do ... at least it hadn't been once Zac had kissed her.

His lips on hers drove all other thoughts right from her mind.

His lips—

The gleam from Babs's ring brought Markie back to the present.

Babs's ring.

She smiled and took her friend's hand, holding it closer so she could truly take it in.

"Is that what I think it is?" Markie asked, admiring the diamond solitaire.

Danny smiled as he rose and embraced Markie. "She said yes."

"I realized that you were right," Babs said. "It wasn't me that was the problem in my other relationships. I just hadn't found the right man."

Babs stood and hugged her, too.

Her mom and Mrs. Marshall rose and joined in.

Then her dad.

Even Zac entered the hugfest, slapping Danny on the back.

Soon, they were all laughing and talking, one over the other.

"So, of course we need to celebrate," her mother said. "Babs's parents are meeting us there, and Bella and..."

Her mom listed pretty much their entire Port Richmond neighborhood.

"Celebrating? Was there ever any question? So, where are we going?" she asked.

"Captain Nemo's," Babs said, grinning.

Markie was just about bursting, seeing her friend so happy. And Danny, her mother, her father... they were all riding high.

She felt about ready to burst with happiness herself.

Her brother and her best friend.

"I called ahead and got a cake," her mom said, adding to the general sweetness of the night.

Markie grinned.

Life was good.

"So, Danny," she asked, as they all filed out of her house, "does this finally get me off the hook for the whole losing you at the Smithsonian thing?"

He kissed her cheek. "Yeah, I guess it does."

Markie gave him a quick hug, but her eyes were on Zac.

Yes, life was very, very good right now.

11

"So…" Markie said when they arrived home at about one.

They'd closed out Nemo's.

Pretty much the whole Port Richmond neighborhood.

Heck, practically all of northeastern Philly.

As Zac closed the front door, some of Markie's euphoria bled away and suddenly, she was nervous.

She took off her coat.

He took off his.

They stood a moment.

Markie didn't quite know what to say.

Part of her didn't want to say anything. That part wanted to simply drag Zac back upstairs and take him to bed.

The other part was nervous and unsure.

She wasn't sure how to act with a friend who'd crossed over to lover.

A friendly lover who was living with her. Only one thin wall separating her room from his.

"Ah…" she hemmed and hawed for a moment, then added, "that was fun."

"You seem nervous," Zac said, standing so close that she could feel him exhale, a soft tickle of air.

He reached over and brushed a piece of hair off her face, a casual sort of intimacy.

She took a quick step back, putting some distance between them. "I'm not nervous exactly. It's just that I think it would be a good idea if we clarify things."

Yes, clarifying.

That was good.

They needed to set down some ground rules, figure out just what the whole we-slept-together thing meant.

"Why don't you let me take you to your room," he said, closing the distance between them and touching her face again. "Come to bed and I'll clarify it for you all night long."

"That's the thing. Earlier, what we did...well, it was good." She saw his sensual smile fade and his face start to darken, that tiny furrow in his brow deepened.

"Great even," she added. "It's just that, I think we need to take a step back...take time to decide if that's the direction we want to go in."

Even as she said the words she realized that stepping back wasn't what she wanted in her heart of hearts. What she wanted was simply to step into his arms. She wanted to stop worrying, damn the consequences and spend the rest of the night wrapped in Zac.

"I don't need time to tell you what I want. You. I want you, Markie. Time won't change that."

"But what about what I want?" she asked.

That was the question. Her wants, her emotions ran the spectrum, from one thing to another. She couldn't exactly pinpoint what that was.

She cared for Zac, wanted Zac. But something was holding her back.

Fear?

Markie liked to think of herself as brave, but what if she let herself go and fell for Zac? What would happen if things went wrong? She'd lost her best friend for eleven months—it had been her fault. She'd been embarrassed and had needed someone to blame. Zac had been handy.

But now that they'd moved beyond that she didn't want to risk losing him again.

"What do you want?" he countered.

"That's what I'm saying, I don't know what I want," she said, her frustration coloring her voice.

"Listen, Zac, I could easily fall into this more intimate relationship with you. But, in the end, if it didn't work, I could lose you. You're too important to me to let that happen. My life has been in a constant state of upheaval for the last year. The wedding, starting the business, and just when things started to settle down, I found a dead body, Maury Desanti—"

Something. Something needled at her again.

"—and then you were suddenly back in my life as a friend. And now..."

"And now?"

"It's just too fast. I need time to figure it out. Alone in my own bed. I just want time to think. I'm not saying no to moving into a more intimate relationship with you. I'm just saying I need time. I'm not ready to share my bed with you."

"We could just sleep together. It's already after one. You could just let me hold you," he said.

Sleeping together, as in really sleeping—was intimate. You learned all sorts of things when you actually slept with someone. Did they drool? Snore? Talk in their sleep?

Markie wasn't sure she could share that with Zac yet.

Maybe putting the brakes on their relationship...maybe that would ensure that no matter what, she'd keep him.

But by the look on his face, maybe not.

She realized he was waiting for an answer.

"Do you really think we could be together in my bed and just sleep?" she asked. "I'm asking for time, Zac."

"Time. You want time. You want to sleep alone? No problem." Zac walked up the stairs and into the guest room, slamming the door.

Ah, that went well.

Depressed, Markie headed to the kitchen. This was a job for... Ho Hos. But as she stared at the box she realized even chocolate cakes couldn't make her feel better.

She was falling into a rut. She grabbed an apple instead. There.

She went back into her room and tried not to think about Zac as she bit into the firm, tart fruit.

It was hard.

Boy, had it been hard...

Gutter mind, she scolded herself.

Forget about Zac.

Think about her poor dead body. Maury Desanti.

The sooner they figured out what was up with him, the sooner Zac could leave.

The thought should make her feel better.

It didn't.

Maybe she didn't want Zac to leave.

Maybe she didn't want to be just friends.

Maybe...

Poor Maury Desanti, she thought as she took another bite.

The feeling that something should click hit her again.

Did she have a Maury on her customer list?

She didn't think so. But maybe she'd done a job for him before he moved into Manchester.

She went to her small desk and opened her laptop.

She opened her business files.

She hit search... *Desanti.*

Nada.

She tried *Maury.*

Still nothing.

She closed the program down.

She was also no closer to figuring out what happened to Maury, and no closer to not thinking about Zac.

She'd sent him to his own room because she was afraid.

Afraid this was going too fast. Afraid she'd end up losing him.

Some people could keep sex casual, but she couldn't, and she was pretty sure neither could Zac. If they made this new facet of their relationship permanent and it didn't work...fear bubbled up inside her at the thought.

Markie wasn't the type to let fear stand in the way of her doing anything. But she simply couldn't make herself go next door to Zac, despite the fact she wanted to.

More than anything, she wanted to.

Maury, she told herself again. *Think about poor Maury Desanti.*

Zac couldn't sleep.

He tossed and turned.

He fumed and he worried.

He spent a great deal of time staring at the wall that separated the guest room from Markie's room.

He should be on her side of that wall right now. Couldn't she see that?

He wanted to march in and tell her, but he forced himself to stay in the guest room and to stay immobile on the lumpy mattress on her guest bed.

He was going to be patient and give her time to realize how right they were for each other.

Yes, he'd be patient even if it killed him.

And if the way he felt tonight as he tossed and turned, trying to find a comfortable position, even though he knew the mattress wasn't the true source of his discomfort...if this was any indication, waiting might very well kill him.

Zac thought he was done waiting after they made love, but here he was, waiting again.

Now he knew what he'd been missing and it was worse.

He glanced at the clock.

Two-thirty.

He had to get some sleep.

He turned and tried to get comfortable. Suddenly, he heard a creak out in the hall.

Just one little *erreeek*.

The sound was out of place.

Someone was out there.

Given everything that had happened at Markie's, Zac wasn't taking any chances. He crept gently out of the bed, careful not to let it make any noise.

Then he walked as quickly as he could to the bedroom door, slowly twisted the handle, and pulled it open.

"Who's out there," he cried, as he sprang into the hall.

A shriek was his only response.

A woman's shriek.

Markie's shriek.

She walked up and thwapped him on the chest.

"What are you doing?" she yelled.

"Investigating," he said.

A small night-light in the hall was enough that he could make out Markie's thin nightgown.

Very thin.

He wanted to reach out and see just how thin it was, but kept his hands firmly at his sides. He was giving her time.

Oh, yeah, the waiting was definitely killing him, but she'd have to make the next move.

"I heard a noise," he continued. "With everything that's happened, I came to investigate."

"You came out here to give me a heart attack," she grumbled.

"What were you doing in the hall at this time of night?"

"Coming to you—"

Those three words were all he needed. His waiting was over, and his heart practically surged out of his chest.

Zac closed the short distance between them in a step and had her in his embrace.

"Zac," she said as a preamble to something else.

But he didn't want to hear anything else.

She'd been coming to him; that was enough.

She'd worked it all out in her mind and realized they should be together.

He pressed his lips to hers, silencing her. He didn't need her apology. He didn't need anything other than her. He deepened the kiss, needing to be closer.

He was delighted when she started kissing him back, joining her lips to his in earnest.

Their clothes were barriers.

He reached for her nightgown and she groaned. Then suddenly, she pulled back. "Zac, stop one minute. I came to tell you I know what's been bothering me since we found Mr. Desanti's body."

He almost groaned at the loss of contact. His breath came in short, tight bursts as he tried to focus on what she'd said.

"Body?" he asked, his brain feeling thick and useless.

"Something's been plaguing me all night."

He'd been tossing and turning, thinking about her, dreaming about her, and she'd been thinking about the name of a corpse?

"Maury Desanti's plagued you all night?" he asked.

"Yes," she said, straightening her nightgown. "I mean, something sounded familiar right from the start. I checked my client list but couldn't come up with why it sounded so familiar."

"And now you know?" he asked.

"Yes." Markie nodded. "Mrs. Sullivan."

"Who?" What the hell was she talking about? He couldn't seem to wrap his brain around whatever it was. He was still stuck on the fact he'd been waiting for her, and she'd been thinking about a corpse's name.

"And?" he asked.

"After the second time I found the body, she said she had an appointment at Manchester Retirement Home—that's where he lived, where you found his body."

"And?"

"She lives next door to me and was home each time we found the body, and that second time we found Maury, she was going to an appointment where he lived."

"I think you're really stretching it."

"We need to go ask her," Markie insisted. "It's our first clue other than the scrap of cloth, which in the end led nowhere."

"It's two-thirty in the morning."

It was two-thirty and he'd been tossing and turning, while Markie was playing Nancy Drew, girl detective, and looking for clues.

"So, we'll go first thing in the morning," she said, insistent.

"You just want to waltz into your neighbor's home and say, *By the way, Mrs. Sullivan, did you know Maury Desanti?*"

"Think about it," she demanded. "It would explain a lot. Why he was on my front porch. She thought I'd left, but I was late that day. She took him in the house while I called 911."

Suddenly, some of the fog cleared from his brain and he was thinking. Thinking like a cop.

Mrs. Sullivan.

Markie's neighbor.

Right next door.

"It would explain why he was in the backyard," Zac mused. "She kept him in the shed for the week, then was going to move him Monday, thinking you'd left, and the other neighbor was at the beauty salon—"

"But I came back for tools," Markie said.

"And when you ran in to call me—"

"She hid him somewhere. Maybe her house, or the trunk of her car. She was parked in the driveway. Not every older lady could handle it, but Mrs. Sullivan is extremely fit. I've seen her carry in groceries. She really loads up the bags and doesn't seem to notice the weight. I think she could handle the body. Maury looked sort of small. I don't know what the motive was, but I'll ask her." Markie smiled. "All I know is I'm not crazy."

"But why wouldn't she have called the police?" he asked. "The coroner said Desanti died of natural causes."

"I don't know." Markie grinned. "But if I'm right, then there is no madman running around my neighborhood."

"And you won't need me staying with you," Zac said. That's what this was all about, her wanting to get rid of him again.

"Zac…"

He shook his head. "It's all right. Don't explain. This isn't your problem."

"Of course it's my problem. You're my friend."

Friend.

The word hit hard.

"Friend," he murmured. "Yeah, I'm your friend."

He could be patient until hell froze over, but it looked like her friendship was all he was ever going to have.

What they'd had earlier was just some aberration.

"Zac," she began again.

He shook his head. He didn't want her pity. He wanted her. But it didn't appear she wanted him.

"Go back to sleep, Markie. We'll go over in the morning. I know she likes to watch that morning show, so she's up early."

"Okay."

He turned and started back into the guest room, but she said his name and he turned back to her. "What?"

"I am your friend, and I hope no matter what happens, you'll continue to be mine."

He sighed as he looked at the hurt in her expression.

"Markie, I'll always be your friend. I'll always be there for you. No matter what happens." It was a promise he felt confident making.

She let out a long breath. "Good."

Good? Zac thought as he closed the door, knowing Markie was just on the other side of that wall.

But she might as well be on the moon.

She didn't feel for him what he felt for her.

He crawled into the cold, narrow bed.

Oh, he'd survive. He'd managed it when he thought he'd lost her to Joel; he'd manage it now.

But he knew he wasn't going to manage it in time to get any sleep tonight.

12

Markie tossed and turned the rest of the night.

Why didn't she just admit she was scared? Zac would have understood.

That was the thing about Zac ... he'd always understood her, even when she didn't understand herself.

But she'd left the words unsaid.

She'd gone back to her own room, when all she really wanted to do was go with him.

To be with him.

By leaving the words unsaid, she'd hurt him.

She hadn't meant to, but she had.

Marquette Ann Walkowicz had hurt tough-man Zachary Marshall and in doing so, she'd hurt herself.

It was about six-thirty when she admitted defeat and finally gave up trying to sleep.

She went down to the kitchen to make coffee.

They'd confront Mrs. Sullivan and when that was done, Markie was going to have to confront her fears and admit to Zac just what she was feeling.

She tried to catalog all her emotions in her mind.

Scared spitless.

Excited.

She felt friendship toward him. That would never change.

But there was something more to her feelings for Zac.

In addition to friendship, there was something deeper. It wasn't something new. Rather, it was a feeling she'd kept buried until now.

Today, she was going to admit to Zac that she—

He walked into the room. His feet were bare. He had on a well-worn pair of jeans and a tight black T-shirt. His hair was wet. He must have showered.

Markie paused, coffee cup midway between the counter and her mouth.

He looked yummy.

Coffee and Zac.

The perfect morning combination.

He looked at her. "What?"

"Morning," she managed to rasp out.

Zac grunted his response as he headed to the cupboard where she stored her cups.

"About last night…" She couldn't wait until after they confronted Mrs. Sullivan. She needed to tell him how she felt now, before she exploded with the hugeness of it.

She was going to confess that things were moving too fast, that she'd been scared, but she realized she had feelings for him.

Feelings?

Okay, so if she was going to be honest, she should probably just tell him that she was pretty sure she loved him.

"I … ah …"

"Forget last night," he said, his voice sharp. "Let's concentrate on this morning."

"But—"

"Not now, Markie. We need to wrap this case up."

"Mrs. Sullivan," Markie said with a sigh.

"Yes," he said, pouring himself a cup of coffee. "Let's see if your hunch is on target."

"But about last night—"

"Leave it, Markie."

His voice was hard and brooked no more arguments.

Zac didn't get stubborn often, but when he did, he was immovable. And he obviously felt rather stubborn over the whole last-night discussion.

"Fine. I'll leave it…" for now, she added silently.

Before the day was out, she was going to tell Zachary Marshall that she loved him.

What he decided to do with the information was up to him. She just knew she wasn't going to let her fear of being hurt keep her silent any longer.

At eight o'clock, they walked across the porch to Mrs. Sullivan's door.

They'd eaten breakfast and after a few uncomfortable minutes, they'd talked about the mundane.

About Danny and Babs.

About their moms.

About Manning.

About anything and everything except last night.

Now, standing outside her neighbor's, Markie wondered if maybe she'd been mistaken. Really. Thinking sweet Mrs. Sullivan had been carting a body around the yard for a week.

"Maybe I'm wrong," she said.

"There's only one way to find out."

Zac knocked on the door.

"Here we go," Markie muttered.

The door flew open. Mrs. Sullivan didn't look pleased to see them.

"Yes?" she asked, punctuating the question with a huge why-me sort of sigh.

"Mrs. Sullivan, may we come in?" Markie asked.

"I'm watching television," she said grumpily. "I don't like anything interrupting my morning show."

"I know, but it's important," Zac said.

Mrs. Sullivan heaved an even bigger, why-me sort of sigh and allowed them in the house.

"Now, what can I do for you?" she asked as she sat in her recliner.

She gave a nod toward the couch and Markie sat down on one end. Rather than sitting in the middle, next to her, Zac sat on the other side, as far from her as he could get and still be on the couch.

Now she was the one sighing, rather than poor TV-deprived Mrs. Sullivan. Talking to Zac later wasn't going to be easy. He was annoyed.

Not that she blamed him.

But still.

"I have a few more questions," Zac said, breaking her train of thought.

"Yes?" Mrs. Sullivan said.

"It's about Maury. We know everything," Markie said, ignoring the dirty look Zac shot her.

"I ... he ..."

Mrs. Sullivan's lip started to quiver.

"Mrs. Sullivan," Markie said as she moved from the couch next to the older lady's chair. She knelt there and put a hand on her arm. "Tell us about why you were going to Manchester Retirement Home last week—about Maury."

"I don't—" Mrs. Sullivan stopped short and stared at both of them. "All right, I confess. I killed him."

"You didn't kill him. It was natural causes. The coroner said he died of a major aneurysm," Zac said, his voice as soft as Markie's had been.

"It might have been natural causes, but it was still my fault. He just… we just… You see, Maury was my boyfriend. We had an… intimate relationship." Some color came back into Mrs. Sullivan's cheeks as she blushed.

"And that day?" Markie prompted.

"It was afterward. We'd both fallen asleep and I woke up and asked if he'd like some supper, but he wouldn't wake up. That's when I realized that he wasn't ever going to wake up again."

"Why didn't you call 911?" Zac asked.

"He was long gone by then. They couldn't have helped and I…" She paused. "I killed him. I guess I got scared. I'm seventy-two—I wouldn't want to get arrested. What would I do in prison? I don't knit and even if I learned, I doubt they'd let me have knitting needles. And heaven knows what I'd look like in one of those uniforms."

Markie and Zac exchanged looks and then Zac cleared his throat. "Uh, right. So maybe you could fill us in on what happened then, Mrs. Sullivan?"

"Well, I decided to just take him to the retirement home and leave him there. I waited until everyone should have left the neighborhood for the day. It was a Monday morning and I knew—"

"That the neighborhood would be deserted," Zac filled in.

Mrs. Sullivan nodded. "Even Gladys leaves early on Mondays. She gets her hair done, then goes to the Senior Bingo Brunch to meet men."

"Ah, that's where she goes," Zac muttered.

"But you," Mrs. Sullivan continued, looking at Markie, "were late. I thought you'd gone, but you hadn't. I'd moved Maury onto the porch and found out he was heavier than I thought. So put him behind the bushes on the porch so no passing cars would see him and went to back my car up as close as I could get."

"But I came out and tripped over him."

"Yes," Mrs. Sullivan nodded. "I'd just spotted your car when I heard you scream. I peeked up and saw you just staring at his body, sort of in a daze. You looked at the bushes, and I ducked back around the house so you wouldn't see me if you looked. I heard the door slam when you went back into the house."

"To call 911," Markie said.

Mrs. Sullivan nodded. "I ran back up and pulled Maury into my place."

"Why didn't you try to take him out again on Friday?" Zac asked. "You said Mrs. Galing got her hair done on Mondays and Fridays."

"Because you'd been around all week. I was too afraid. I moved Maury into the shed to keep him cold. I waited until Markie told me you'd given up before I decided it was safe to move him again. I waited for the next Monday. I was dragging him from the shed right to my car—"

"And I came back for tools," Markie said.

"So I managed to get him into the trunk of my car."

"And then we came over and you had that appointment," Zac said.

"Yes." Mrs. Sullivan shook her head. "It's a relief to tell someone. I felt horrible. I'll miss Maury. He was a good man."

She thrust her hands out at Zac. "So, go ahead and cuff me. Take me to jail. Throw away the key. I'm a murderer."

Markie patted the woman's arm and looked at Zac to see what he was going to do.

"You're not a murderer," he said, not moving from his place on the couch. "Actually, moving the body is the only thing you did that was illegal. Abuse of corpse."

"Oh, no," Mrs. Sullivan cried. "That sounds even worse."

"But you know, the D.A. would laugh this out of his office if I took a charge like that to him," Zac said.

"Laugh?" Mrs. Sullivan said in a weepy sort of voice.

"If I'm not mistaken, the charge is a simple misde-meanor. And given that no one was hurt by it…"

"The court system is so overloaded with real criminals," Markie added, shooting him a smile.

Zac nodded. "I just don't see the point in pursuing this."

"You mean I'm not under arrest?" Mrs. Sullivan asked weakly.

"No. But," Zac said, his voice getting stern, "if anything bad ever happens to you again with one of your *friends*, you have to call 911 and report it right away."

"I will," she promised. "And Markie, honey, I'm so sorry this scared you."

"I'm just relieved knowing there's no murderer lurking around Port Richmond."

"Well, then," said Mrs. Sullivan, looking a bit more like herself. "Now what?"

"Now," Zac said, "Markie and I have some business of our own to settle."

"I don't know how to thank you," Mrs. Sullivan said.

"Just don't let it happen again." Zac's voice was suddenly all cop-tough.

"I won't," she promised as she followed them to the door.

Markie and Zac walked across the porch to her house.

"That was a nice thing you did," she said as they shut the door.

"Not nice. Practical. I meant what I said—the D. A. would have laughed any charges right out of his office. There was no point dragging Mrs. Sullivan's name into court."

"Still, it was nice."

He started to walk up the stairs.

"Where are you going?" she asked.

"Home," he said. "We've solved the mystery. There's no reason for me to stay."

"About last night," Markie started, unsure how to say what she had to say.

She wanted to say, *stay*, but she couldn't make the words come out of her mouth.

She wanted to say, *I'm scared, but I think I have feelings for you.*

She wanted so much, but no sound came out.

"You've made yourself pretty clear," Zac said. "I think it's best if I go."

"But—"

"Listen, Markie, you said it yourself. Things have moved fast. Too fast. I want you. Don't get me wrong, I want you, that hasn't changed. That will never change. But I'm not going to rush you. I'm willing to wait."

She had time. He'd wait.

"For how long?" she asked.

"However long you need. I didn't go anywhere in the last eleven months of waiting, and that's not going to change. I'll wait. You come to me when you're ready."

"What if I said I'm ready now?"

That's what she wanted to say if only she could find a way to force the words past the fear clogging her throat.

She'd thought she'd loved someone once before and it had ended badly. Now, she didn't even miss Joel.

But Zac?

Zac, she'd miss.

"If you said the words now, I'd call you a liar."

"But—"

"Think about it, Markie. Think long and hard. Because when you come to me, it will be for keeps. There will be no going back."

"No going back," she repeated.

"Never. So be sure. Be very sure."

Zac forced himself to leave her there in the front hall and walk up the stairs to the guest room. He packed his bag. It was the hardest thing he'd ever done.

But she had to be sure. Because he couldn't lose her again.

When he returned, Markie was standing in the center of the living room still looking lost.

"Zac," she said. "I …"

"I know. Take your time. I'll be here." He kissed her cheek. Soft, wanting to linger, but not daring to.

"I'll talk to you soon," he said and hefted his bag and walked out the door, leaving the woman he loved behind.

13

Two days later, there was a knock on the door.

Markie figured she'd ignore it, just like she'd ignored all the other knocks and calls at home over the last two days.

She wished she'd done the same at work. But no, she'd gone through the motions and dealt with the other receptionist hopefuls her mother had sent.

The most likely candidate had stated, "And your mother said you were open to a flexible schedule. That would be perfect for me. I can't work Mondays because I have tai chi, then Tuesdays are..."

The woman continued listing the details comprising her schedule until Markie finally interrupted. "Just when would you be available to work?"

"Wednesday mornings and Thursday after lunch."

It wasn't much, but Mrs. Clarence at least had nominal experience using a computer and was the cream of the crop as far as applicants went. Markie eventually decided that avoiding the office was the way to go. However, maybe she shouldn't have...at least her mom's candidates distracted Markie from her Zac quandary.

After all, there wasn't a whole lot that could keep her from thinking about Zac.

Her mind kept chasing after itself—wanting Zac, but afraid to go after him, afraid that it might not work, afraid that in the end she might lose him.

She'd always thought she was brave, but over the last two days she'd discovered she was a coward.

There was more knocking.

She didn't get up.

But whoever it was didn't go away. She heard the door open, then close.

Markie vowed she was going to get a new dead bolt and not give anyone the key. She'd never leave it unbolted.

Her mother, her brother, Babs... Zac. They all had keys.

She prayed it would be Zac walking into the living room. That the next move would be taken out of her hands.

She tried to bite back the disappointment she felt when Babs came into the living room.

"You look like hell," her friend said.

"Gee, thanks," Markie muttered between a bite of Ho Ho. "You look radiant."

"That's what love will do to you." She paused a moment and added, "Radiant or hellish... I don't think there's any middle ground with love."

Markie didn't say anything, mainly because she didn't know what to say.

"You know," Babs said, plopping down on the couch next to her, helping herself to a Ho Ho, "I know how you feel."

"No, you don't."

No one could. Wants, fears, desire, excitement, doubts... all mingled and left her feeling paralyzed.

"Sweetie, I know you and Zac... well, you've taken the relationship up a notch from friendship. I knew it when we showed up at your house to announce our engagement. Zac might have started out in the guest room, but that's not where he ended up. Really, I understand what it's like moving from friends to friends-with-benefits."

She paused and added with a smile, "And from the way you radiated contentment that night, I'm thinking the benefits were pretty beneficial with Zac."

"They were," Markie admitted, with a ghost of a smile on her face. "But afterward..." She shook her head. "You don't get it."

"Yes, I do. You're torn. Torn between your fears and..." She paused.

"And?"

"And you're in love," Babs said.

"I never said I was in love," Markie said. At least, she hadn't said it out loud.

"You didn't have to," Babs assured her. "You have all the signs. You're despondent, you're chowing down on sweets— and you and I both know Ho Hos are your comfort food. Add to that, you look like hell and... well, you've either got a deadly illness or you're in love."

"I think a deadly illness would be easier," Markie said.

"What I don't understand is what are you so afraid of?" Babs asked as she unwrapped the sweet. "I was scared of what people would say, what they'd think of me dating a younger man."

She sighed and took a huge bite.

"That was a lie," she said, her mouth stuffed with Ho Ho. "I was afraid that I'd screw up things with Danny, just like I'd screwed them up with every other man I ever dated."

"You didn't screw them up. The other men... they were nothing."

"I know. But still, Danny mattered so much more than anyone else I'd ever been with. If I'd lost him, I don't know what I'd have done."

Babs took a bite of her Ho Ho, then said, "What you have to ask yourself is not just what you feel for Zac. The question is; can you go on without him? I discovered I couldn't go on without Danny. In the end, my insecurities and fears didn't amount to anything compared to what I'd feel if I had to go on without him."

"It's only been two days and I feel like there's a hole in my life," Markie said. "I've wanted to go to him. He told me to be sure when I did because when I did it was forever. But what if I'm wrong? I mean, I thought I loved Joel and look how that turned out."

"Joel was nothing compared to Zac. And you can *what if* all you want. *What if* I'm wrong, *what if* we don't make it. But truly, what if you aren't wrong? What if you sit around worrying and eventually he gets tired of waiting?

"So what are you going to do?" Babs asked.

"I…"

"Don't over-think it," she said. "Don't hesitate and analyze all the *what ifs* to death. Just tell me, what are you going to do? Sit here eating Ho Hos and feeling like hell, or go after the man you love?"

"I'm going after him," Markie said, her voice barely a whisper.

"What? I couldn't hear you," Babs said, a huge smile on her face.

"I said," Markie said, her voice louder, her doubts falling to the side, "I'm going after him."

"So what are you doing here stuffing Ho Hos in your mouth with me?" Babs asked. "You've got a man out there waiting for you."

"I don't know."

"So, go already."

Markie started toward the stairs. She needed a shower, and some makeup and—

Babs's voice stopped her. "Oh, before you go, I actually came here for something."

Markie turned and asked, "What?"

"Will you be maid of honor at my wedding?"

They both stared at each other a moment and then burst into tears.

"This calls for a toast," Markie said.

"It's only ten."

"Hey, you're in love and I'm in love." The words felt right... they felt sweet as she said them. "And I'm in love," she said again just because she suddenly could. "I don't think it matters what time it is. It's time for a toast."

They were both laughing as they headed to the kitchen.

Markie stared at her refrigerator. No wine. No beer. She pulled out two diet colas.

"Best I could do," she said apologetically.

"It's fine. Everything's fine. The world is a beautiful place," Babs crooned.

They were both laughing as they pulled the tabs and toasted.

"To the men we love." Clink. Chug.

"To best friends." Clink. Chug.

"To Ho Hos." Clink. Chug.

"To Port Richmond." Clink. Chug.

They toasted and clinked their way through their cans, then went for a second one each.

Ho Hos, cola and a good friend—Markie figured the only thing that would make life better was a good man... and she planned on going for hers next.

❦ ❦ ❦

Zac was on his way out to the parking lot. He'd finished the shift and wished he hadn't. He wished he had an active case, something that would require him to put in overtime.

But he didn't and it was time to head home to a quiet house.

That's when it got to him—when it was quiet. When he was alone.

He wanted Markie.

Two days.

When he'd made his grand exit, he thought she'd think about it for a while—say, five minutes—then come to her senses. But here it was two days later and she still hadn't come to him. Hadn't phoned.

Nothing.

Nada.

Just that empty house waiting for him.

He wanted to go to Markie's place and shake some sense into her.

What had he been thinking? This whole giving-her-time idea wasn't the best one he'd ever come up with.

What he should have done was take her to bed and keep her there until she realized that there was no place she'd rather be.

Until she realized that they were meant to be together.

Until she realized she loved him as much as he loved her.

Yeah, he thought as he reached his car. He should have skipped being noble and gone for what he wanted.

And what he wanted was Markie Walkowicz.

It's what he'd always wanted.

"Hey, Marshall," Matt Manning called, heading across the parking lot to join him. "So what's your crazy girlfriend doing now that you've found her corpse?"

He shrugged. "I don't know."

He didn't have a clue and it was killing him. Now that they'd figured out the mystery behind the disappearing body, was that it? He'd helped her and now she could go on with her life...a life that didn't include him.

He couldn't figure her out.

They were good together. How could she not see it? They were meant for each other, even. But she wouldn't admit it.

He'd given her time.

Two whole days.

Forty-eight hours.

Practically a lifetime.

But she hadn't come by.

Hadn't phoned.

She'd probably gotten on with her life. Building her business, hanging out with her family.

She'd probably forgotten all about him, just like she had for eleven months.

Well, Zac had learned his lesson. Walkowiczes got strange notions and could stubbornly cling to them for a long time. For some reason, Markie had come to the conclusion there were obstacles standing in their way.

Well, he wasn't going to stand for it. He was going to convince her that there was nothing they couldn't overcome. Missing corpses, their mothers...nothing.

"So what are you going to do?" Manning asked.

He was going to go after Markie, but that's not what Manning was asking.

"About the case?" Zac asked, checking he was still in tune with whatever Manning was talking about.

Manning nodded.

"Nothing. The coroner said Desanti died of natural causes, so there's no case. It's over."

But over didn't describe what he and Markie had between them.

He'd given her two days. Before that, he'd given her eleven months to heal and come to her senses. He'd been patient.

To be honest, Markie could test the patience of a saint.

And Zac was no saint.

He was done waiting.

If Mohammed wouldn't come to the mountain, well, the mountain was going to her.

"Hey, when you talk to Markie, tell her I'm sorry, okay?" Manning said.

Zac knew he'd be waiting a long time to talk to Markie if she had her way. She'd taken eleven months to talk to him again after her almost wedding, and then she'd only talked to him because she needed him.

He couldn't wait another eleven months.

Couldn't even wait another eleven hours.

The mountain was on its way to Markie Walkowicz's house, whether she was ready to admit what they had or not.

"Yeah, sure I'll deliver the message," he said.

He'd deliver it all right, along with a message of his own.

"Port Richmond," Markie said. Clink. Chug.

"I think you already said that," Babs said.

"Maybe, but it needs to be said again. The best of everything comes from Port Richmond. The best friends. The best family. Even though my mom drives me nuts, she's the best. The best men."

"To the best men," Babs said. Clink. Chug. "That's the end of my second cola. I'm pretty sure that's my limit for the day."

"Party pooper," Markie said.

"I think you're stalling."

"Maybe. Either I have nervous butterflies in my stomach, or two colas before lunch is two too many."

"Well, I'm friend enough to tell you it won't work," Babs said. "Once a man gets to you like Danny got to me, or Zac's gotten to you, stalling doesn't help. Thinking doesn't help because you can't think…men like that take up all the space in your brain." She nudged the box of Ho Hos. "Even chocolate—which can solve almost any problem known to womankind—won't work. There's only one thing to do."

"What?" Markie asked, though she knew the answer.

"Find your man, tell him how it is, that you love him and he's just going to have to learn to live with it. Then take him to bed and have your way with him."

"Having my way with Zac does sound like a plan." She grinned. Oh, yeah, having her way with him was quite an appealing idea.

"So, I ask again, what are you still doing here?" Babs asked, laughing.

"I'm going to go shower, then I'll be on my way to find Zac and tell him how it is."

"Good for you," Babs cheered.

"And when I'm done telling him I love him and he's stuck with me, I'll have my way with him."

"Hear, hear."

"I'll—"

The doorbell rang.

"I'm going to get the door," Markie said, "then I'm going to get my man."

"Yeah!"

Feeling powerful and in control for the first time in about eleven months, Markie walked to the front door. She was going to get rid of whoever it was and then she was going to find Zac.

She opened the door and smiled.

She wasn't going to have to look too hard for Zac, because there he was, on her porch. No happy smile hello. As a matter of fact, he was scowling.

"Hey, Zac," she said, wishing she'd prettied up, but knowing he'd seen her looking worse and never seemed to mind.

"We're going to talk and we're going to talk now," he said, walking into the hall and kicking the door shut behind him in a totally he-man, tough cop sort of way.

"I was just—" she started.

He interrupted, "I don't care what you were just doing. You're going to sit down and listen to what I have to say."

He didn't wait to be invited. He just stomped into the living room, leaving Markie with nothing to do but follow.

He spotted Babs.

"Uh, I was just leaving," she said as she hurried past Zac. When she reached Markie, she gave her a quick kiss on the cheek.

"Go get him," she whispered in Markie's ear.

Markie smiled as Babs rushed out. The door slammed behind her.

"I was just—" Markie started again.

"Quiet. Not a word," Zac said.

Being ordered around, even by the man she loved—*the man she loved*…the words felt so right—didn't sit well with Markie.

"Listen, I'm trying to make allowances," she said. "But there's no way I'm going to let you boss me around like this."

"Sit," he barked, in what Markie could only imagine was his best cop voice. Firm. Commanding. The type of tone no one could argue with.

"I'm only sitting because I feel like sitting," she grumbled as she sat on the couch.

"Now, it's time we talked," he said, as he paced back and forth in front of her.

"I keep trying to talk and you keep yelling at me to be quiet."

"Let me rephrase that." He stopped pacing and stared at her. "It's time I talk and you listen."

"But I want—"

"Shh," he said.

"You know, I don't take orders well."

"This once, you're going to have to, because I've been as patient as I know how to be. I mean it, Markie, I'm the epitome of patience, but you've pushed me beyond even my abilities."

"I—"

He kept right on talking, ignoring the beginning of her comment. "I told you the first time you dated Joel that he was a hound, but you two seemed to be making a go of it. He seemed to have settled down, so I minded my peace. I was happy for you both, at least at first. But slowly, that happiness turned to something else. I realized you were more than a friend. That I had feelings for you. That night before your wedding I didn't know about Joel and the stripper, I just knew I didn't want you to marry him. I wanted to ask you to postpone the wedding, to tell you that I had feelings for you, but I got as far as, *Maybe you shouldn't marry Joel tomorrow*—"

"—and I got mad."

"Just a bit," he said with a small smile. "I never got to the confessing part when you started in on how much you loved him and were so pissed that I'd asked you not to marry him."

"You didn't know he wasn't coming to the wedding?"

"Don't you think I would have told you if I did?"

"Yes. It's just I was so mad, so confused."

"I was confused as well when he didn't show up. I tracked him down and found him with that woman. We discussed things and I expressed my displeasure."

She looked at him. "That's why he had a black eye when he came for his stuff?"

Zac didn't deny or admit anything, but Markie was pretty sure he'd *discussed* things with Joel just like he'd *discussed* them with Stan Phillips all those years ago.

"You said you came to tell me you had feelings for me. What kind of feelings?" she asked.

"Love," he said. "I loved you then ... and now."

"Why didn't you tell me the truth?"

"I felt guilty. Guilty because I was relieved you'd finally learned the truth about Joel before it was too late. Guilty because it hurt you and because I had this insane hope that maybe you'd learn to see me as more than a friend."

"Instead you ended up on my least-liked list. I needed someone to blame and Joel was in Vegas with his stripper. You'd been right to warn me, which was bad enough. But when I realized that I wasn't crushed to have Joel stand me up at the wedding, that was worse. Because it didn't take me long to figure out that I wasn't even missing him. That made me feel shallow. I didn't miss him, but I did miss you. You know me so well—I didn't want you realizing that I'd fooled myself into thinking I'd loved Joel. I didn't call you because I was embarrassed. Then, the longer I stayed away, the harder it became to face you. I honestly don't think I ever really blamed you for more than a minute and I was wrong to stay away."

"Hell yes, you were wrong."

"I apologize for that."

"I don't want your apology..." His voice lowered as he added, "I just want you. I've always wanted you, even before I realized it. You're a part of me. You're under my skin."

"You're under mine, too." She stood and walked right up to him. Toe to toe. She came to him.

"Quiet," he said, even as his hand reached out and gently brushed against her cheek. "Let me finish this. I know I said I'd be patient and two days doesn't really seem patient on the surface, but if you factor in all the years I waited, you'd have to admit I've been—"

"Here I am," she said, reaching out to move that stray lock of hair that always tumbled into his left eye. She wanted to be sure he could see her, that his view wasn't obstructed.

"Shh."

"You shh. You said you'd wait for me to come to you, but when I did I'd better remember that it was for keeps. Well, here I am. I came to you. Actually, I planned to come all the way to your house for you, but there you were on my doorstep. That was convenient. But even though you were here, you still waited, because you are the soul of patience, and I have indeed come to you."

"You know what you're saying?" he asked.

"Yes. And I hope you do as well, because it's for keeps. There's no going back on it. You're mine. You've always been mine, I've just been too blind to see it."

"You sure were."

"But I see it now."

"Just what do you see?"

"You, standing there, loving me. And I hope you see me, standing here, loving you. I've started a new list, you see."

He groaned. "You and your lists."

"Ah, but this isn't my least-liked list. I've taken you totally off that one, although Manning and Sylvia Carson are still on it. No, this one is new. My most-loved list. You're right at the top."

Suddenly he was grinning. "The top?"

"Number one." She laughed because all the worries and doubts suddenly dissolved and all that was left was the love. "I love you."

"For keeps," he said more than asked.

"For keeps. You always believed in me, even when I doubted myself, you believed." How could she have missed that all these years?

"I loved you," he said. "Believing in you was easy."

"It took me long enough to see it," she said.

"You know what this means?"

"What?"

"Our moms," he said. "Oh, man, can you imagine what they're going to do when they hear?"

"First Danny, now me." Markie shook her head. "I don't know if she'll be able to stand the excitement. The whole Port Richmond brigade will truly come out in force."

"I guess we don't have to tell them right away," Zac murmured.

"No, not right away. I think there's something we should do first," Markie said. "And I think it might take a while."

"A very long while," Zac said, pulling her toward the stairs.

Laughing, Markie followed him.

EPILOGUE

Markie spotted her quarry across the reception hall. "Come on. There he is."

"Markie," her husband said with a warning tone to his voice.

"Don't worry. It's all right."

"I am worried. You've had wilder ideas than normal lately."

"Like what?" she asked.

"Like hiring Mrs. Sullivan as your receptionist."

"That wasn't wild, that was smart. It gets her out of the house and keeps her away from trouble. And she was the most qualified person I met with. It's a win-win situation. Come on, let's go before he gets away."

"Before who gets away?" Veronica—Ronnie—Hastings, Babs's cousin and one of the other bridesmaids, asked. "And who's Mrs. Sullivan?"

Babs had asked Markie to be maid of honor, but had gladly settled for *matron* of honor after Markie and Zac's quickie wedding.

Zac had pushed for the shortest engagement in history. He claimed he'd waited long enough.

Markie sighed as she looked at how good Zac, Danny's best man, looked in his tux.

"Who?" Ronnie asked again.

Markie pulled her thoughts from her husband of three weeks and forced herself to think of her plan.

"Someone I want you to meet," she told Ronnie.

Babs's cousin looked worried. "Markie, I don't know."

"Trust me."

"I've heard stories about your escapades from my cousin."

"Babs exaggerates." Ronnie didn't look as if she was buying it. "Come on, before he gets away."

She dragged the very reluctant Ronnie toward her quarry.

"Hey, Matt," she called happily.

"Oh, no," the young cop groaned and started toward the door. "You've got that look in your eyes. You're up to something. Listen, I've apologized a hundred times. I even gave you a toaster oven for a wedding gift. I should be off the list by now."

"You are," Markie promised. Being married had mellowed her. She'd let everyone but Sylvia Carson off the list.

"I'm not here to do anything to you," she promised.

"Ha!" he scoffed.

"I'm here to introduce you to someone."

"I don't want to—"

"Matt Manning, meet Ronnie Hastings."

Matt sighed his defeat and nodded at Ronnie, who didn't look any more enthused than he did.

"Matt used to be a closet romance reader, but then I outed him."

"See, there you go," he said. "And that was a top-of-the-line toaster oven. The lady at the store guaranteed it would impress you."

"It did. This is me paying you back. You see, Ronnie is—"

"You read romance?" Ronnie asked. "I work at Byers Books. I'm in charge of the fiction department. Did you know that more than half the books we sell are romance?"

"Really?" Matt asked.

"Oh, yeah. Most of our regulars are romance readers. Do you read—"

The two of them started talking books, but Markie didn't get a chance to join in because Zac was pulling her onto the dance floor. "Come on, you've done your part."

"I think they're going to hit it off," she said, as he pulled her close and swayed to the music.

"I think you need to stop worrying about them and should start worrying about your husband."

"Oh, does my husband have a problem?"

"Not when he's holding you," Zac murmured against her ear as he pulled her even tighter.

All thoughts of Matt and Ronnie, and even Danny and Babs, evaporated.

The only thoughts that were left were of Zac.

Her husband.

Her best friend.

And that was more than enough.

I hope you enjoyed Markie's mystery…and romance.

If you did, please leave a review so others can find it too!

As always, thank you for picking up my book. I hope you'll come find me on social media. There are links on my website www.HollyJacobs.com.

Holly Jacobs

PS Looking for another who-dunnit? Meet Quincy Mac, a maid in LA who accidentally cleaned a murder scene…and has to find the killer before she goes to jail for a murder she only cleaned! Turn the page…I've included the opening to Steamed: A Maid in LA Mystery book 1.

STEAMED: A MAID IN LA MYSTERY

HOLLY JACOBS

CHAPTER ONE

When I moved to la, I was an eighteen year old with stars in my eyes. Well, not exactly in my eyes, but rather *on* my eyes. My high school best friend bought me sunglasses with lenses shaped like stars for when I *Made It.* Lottie always said the words in such a way you just knew they were capitalized.

Made It.

Yes, I graduated from high school and moved to LA. I planned to be a famous actress. Lottie made me promise I'd wear my star-shaped glasses on my first Oscar red carpet walk. My goal was to take Hollywood by storm.

These days, those glasses are in a drawer in my bedroom and I have two much smaller goals. One is that I want to wear my jeans without a muffin-top. After three kids, I'd developed a bit of a baby-pooch that wants to creep out above the waistband of my jeans. I longed for the days when pants had waistbands that were higher. Back then you could tuck your baby-pooch in. These days your options are exercise, wear Spanx, or learn to suck it in.

I tend to suck it in … when I remember.

My second goal is an empty nest.

It's not that I don't love my boys. I do. I have three sons—Hunter, Miles and Eli. They are eighteen, seventeen and sixteen. I've been a parent practically my entire adult life. I'm ready for a time when I simply have to worry about me and no one else.

This summer is my trial empty-nest.

The boys left last night to spend four weeks in the Bahamas with their father and his most recent wife, Peri.

Now, my place isn't exactly a dump, but compared to their dad's house, my three-bedroom bungalow in the out-of-the-way neighborhood of Van George is a cardboard box in some alley.

And while thirty-eight isn't exactly over-the-hill, next to Peri, the twenty-year-old, I am ancient.

I miss my boys (and I realize the irony in longing for an empty nest, but missing them when they're on vacation). I try not to mind when my ex takes the boys on fabulous vacations—and most of the time I don't mind—but getting ready for work in a quiet house, I minded.

My ex, movie producer Jerome Smith, is a nice guy ... a nice guy with a taste for younger women. Specifically women between the ages of twenty and twenty-five. The exact ages I married, then divorced him. Or rather, he divorced me.

Jerome had two marriages before me, and three marriages since, all within those same parameters. His current wife's my favorite. I really like Peri despite the way her breasts perk and mine just sort of ... well, hang loosely if they're not strapped down. I think Peri sort of appeals to my maternal instincts. I don't have a daughter.

Maybe I'll adopt her when Jerome divorces her.

TGIF, I told myself. I'm thirty-eight, and until the boys come home from their summer visit with their father, I'm footloose and fancy-free.

Maybe it isn't exactly the life I'd dreamed of when I moved to LA, but it's a good life.

Oh, sometimes I still wish that I were starring in some movie of the week instead of heading into Mac'Cleaners.

Yes, that's right—I no longer have stars in or on my eyes. Rather than achieving stardom, I have three sons and clean houses for a living. It's honest work, and it's flexible enough that when I was younger I could take time off and go on auditions. Now that I'm part owner and thirty-eight, I don't go to many auditions.

Okay, so I haven't been on an audition in five years— I've discovered that I'm a size twelve girl in a size two world.

I missed the fame and fortune boat.

Okay, so I could live without fame or fortune, if only I could figure out what I wanted to do with my life sometime before menopause hit. Owning a business keeps the boys and me afloat financially but lately, I'd had a feeling that it was time for a change. The kids weren't such kids anymore. Hunter would start college in the fall.

That empty nest is just around the bend. Soon I'll be able to live my own life.

And I know I want something more.

I'd said I wanted to act since I was six. I never gave any thought to doing something else. But it's clear that acting isn't going to be my ultimate career.

So while I wait to figure out what I want to do, I clean houses. I need to figure out soon because I'll be turning forty in a couple years. Forty sounds so very grown up, and grown-ups should have some idea about the direction they want their lives to take.

But I wasn't going to think about direction today.

Today, I was going to get my work done and then go do something decadent.

I'd like to say I was planning to go to a bar and pick up guys—well at least pick up a guy—but I'll probably end up going to the store and picking up Ben and Jerry's, then head home and try and catch up on all the chick-flicks the boys make me miss.

Feeling a bit better, I walked into the small brick storefront that was only a mile from my house. It proudly proclaimed Mac'Cleaners on the plate glass window with a tartan weaving through the letters. I walked through the small reception room and back to my partner, Tiny's office.

Big mistake.

There's nothing worse than starting the day as a single, directionless, mother of three and then walking into the middle of the wonderful world of weddings.

Tiny's marrying Salvador Mardones in September. September 30th to be exact. And she's going slightly insane...a bit further over the brink each day.

"Tiny?" I called, hoping she was somewhere in the sea of tulle and satin.

"I'm here, Quincy," she said from the back corner.

Tiny's not very...tiny that is. She's five eight and looks like a model. Skin the color of strong tea and dark hair with a tendency to curl. She's gorgeous and simply a beautiful soul. We make an interesting pair, what with me having Irish fair skin, a light sprinkling of freckles that might have been cute when I was in my teens, but aren't as much when at thirty-eight. And my hair...well, it was blond when I moved to LA thanks to Lottie and Miss Clairol. These days, it has gone back to its brownish roots...literally.

Tiny smiled as I walked in, and I couldn't muster up true annoyance that her smile was messing with my grouchy mood because she radiated happiness. The kind of happiness I knew she deserved.

"It's getting worse, isn't it?" she asked, gesturing at her office.

I surveyed the room. "Yeah."

"I just can't help myself. I want this wedding to be perfect because Sal's perfect."

Truth is, Sal is perfect. He's my five five height, balding and has a beer belly that makes my small baby-pooched stomach look like washboard abs.

But he's truly one of the nicest guys in the world.

Tiny had a history of dating losers. But that was over because Sal...well, he's a winner.

"The wedding will be perfect," I promised.

I'd see to it, even though I'd rather have wisdom teeth pulled than plan a wedding this elegant.

Me, if I ever get married again, I'm eloping. Something fast and simple. Someone saying the official words, then my new husband and me back at some hotel having sex. Lots and lots of sex.

It had been a while, which might explain why my mind skipped right over finding Mr. Right and a wedding and went right to the sex.

"Speaking of help," Tiny said slowly, "we need some today. Theresa's out."

Rats.

"It's my turn, isn't it?" I asked, though I knew the answer.

She nodded.

When one of our employees calls in sick, we take turns filling in.

Today it was my turn to fill in.

I should have just gone back to bed this morning.

Grumbling to myself, I left Tiny to hold down the fort and took Theresa's folder for the day. The nice thing about working outside the office is that the day always went fast.

Today was no exception. By three in the afternoon, I was on my way to the last job.

As soon as I finished Mr. Banning's, I'd decided that I was going shopping for a new pair of shoes rather than Ben and Jerry's.

More money, less calories.

I thought the trade-off was worth it.

On a day like today, I didn't just want new shoes—I needed them. So, I grabbed Mr. Banning's printout from Theresa's folder. I was anxious to finish this last job.

Mr. Banning's was a BWP/wL.

A basic-weekly-pickup, with laundry.

I knocked on his door, even though the file said the odds of him being home at three o'clock in the afternoon were slim to nil.

I used our key and let myself in. I surveyed the living room with disgust. There was nothing basic about this job.

The place was a mess.

I mean, a real pigsty. Worse than my boys' rooms...and that's saying something. Teenage boys are very toxic.

Mr. Banning was a whole new level of toxicity, though. Underwear was hanging from a chandelier, empty glasses and plates were scattered through the room.

Oh, geesh. Mr. Banning had a Mortie. All TV Network, ATVN, had begun to hand out the award ten years ago and it had quickly become one of the premier Hollywood awards.

Hey, I might not be an actual actress, but I know stuff.

I noticed not out of some sort of awe that I was cleaning a Mortie winner's home, but rather because the award was sitting in the middle of the leather couch, covered in something. Maybe someone had dipped it into some of the food. Ugh. It looked like they'd tried to wipe it off before throwing it on the couch, but they didn't wipe hard enough.

To top it off, there were footprints on the light beige carpet. Big footprints. Whoever wore those shoes had really big feet. Thankfully, there were only two. As if whoever made the prints realized they'd tracked in mud and took off their shoes, because those two prints were it.

Well, there'd been at least one considerate person.

I tried to make a mental list of how best to approach this job.

In the end, there was nothing to do but start. I gathered dishes and cups and the pots and pans in the kitchen and had the dishwasher running minutes later. I even hand-washed the Mortie—which was about as heavy as a bag of sugar, heavier than I'd thought the old-fashioned silver television would be—and gave it a thorough polish. When I was done, the inscription on the silver television screen really stood out. Steve Banning. *Dead Certain.*

I remembered that show. It was a comedy about a medical examiner's office.

I set the Mortie on the mantle, thinking that was a more appropriate place for it than the couch.

There was a desk next to the fireplace. It had an old relic of a computer on it. The keyboard's cord dangled over the edge of the desk. Yeah, that wasn't going to work well.

I plugged the keyboard into the back of the tower.

Next, I dragged a garbage can around the room and made short order of the rest of the mess.

I debated whether I should toss the chandelier's panties out, but opted to put them in the wash with a load of clothes. At least when Mr. Banning returned them to whoever they belonged to, they'd be clean.

Maybe they belonged to him?

The thought was enough to make me decide to concentrate on the job at hand rather than on the underclothing our Mortie-winning client wore.

There was a small steam-cleaner in the back of the Mac'Cleaners van. It made short work of the footprints. I worked on the laundry as I vacuumed and dusted. By then the dishwasher was finished, so I unloaded it then cleaned the kitchen.

I found the bra that matched the panties under the sink.

Personally, I didn't want to know why there was a bra under the sink. Maybe Mr. Banning had a dishwashing fetish and the mystery naked woman helped him out? The mental image was disturbing.

I knew walking into the place that Mr. Banning liked women.

It said so on his file. Right after BWP/wL it said *DOG*.

That's our code for he liked women a lot and liked a lot of them.

Yes, Mr. Banning is a dog…a letch.

But he never bothers the staff, so it didn't bother us.

Mac'Cleaners is an equal opportunity employee. We stake our reputation on good service and discretion.

This job was going to require a lot of discretion on my part. I wondered if Theresa's illness had anything to do with knowing that Mr. Banning's place was this bad and that she'd have to clean it up?

Kitchen done, I moved onto and finished the bathroom as well. Then I folded a load of laundry and put another one in the dryer. With the job almost done, I was getting excited about shoe shopping, which in LA is a unique treat. So many shoes, so few feet. I headed to Mr. Banning's bedroom.

If his living room was a pit, I really didn't want to know what condition his bedroom was in. Knowing that all that stood between me and some Santee Alley bargain shopping was this bedroom, I opened the door, took all of one step in and…screamed.

It wasn't a frustrated scream.

It wasn't even a this-guy-is-such-a-pig sort of scream.

No, it was more like a there's-a-bloody-dead-body-on-the-bed sort of scream.

Loud, long and more than a little crazed.

I wanted to keep screaming and run right out of the house, but I managed to get myself under control. The killer had to be long gone, or else he—or she—would have attacked me as I cleaned. I was safe. I couldn't say the same for poor Mr. Banning.

I reached in my back pocket, pulled out my cell phone and called 911.

"You've reached Los Angles emergency dispatch."

"I need help," I blurted out.

"What is the nature of your emergency?" the man on the other end of the phone asked.

"Mr. Banning's dead. There's blood on his head and his eyes are open."

Those eyes were going to give me nightmares for the rest of my life.

"Your address ma'am?"

"I'm at, he's at—" I had to think a moment, but then I somehow pulled his address from the fog that was my mind and blurted it out.

"Who are you?" the operator asked.

"I'm the maid. Quincy Mac."

Now, some people prefer the term domestic engineer, or some fancy title. I call it like I see it. I'm a maid.

I had no idea why I thought of what to call myself at that moment. Maybe it was nerves. After all it's not every day I find a dead client.

Thinking about my job description was easier than thinking about those eyes and all that blood.

"Ma'am are you sure he's dead?"

"I don't think there's any way someone could look that bloody and blue and still be breathing."

This was the ultimate topper to my day from hell.

A dead man in the bedroom.

As I talked to the operator, I walked outside. Not really walked, trotted. I moved fast. I mean, no way was I staying in a house with a dead guy.

I was thankful for my cell phone as I stepped out onto the bright sidewalk.

Perfect.

All that LA sunshine made it hard to believe that someone was dead a short distance away.

The emergency operator continued asking me questions. The company's name, my name and address, etc…

Personally, I sort of zoned out. I think I answered him all right but couldn't be sure.

Actually, I didn't want to be sure.

I just wanted to go home.

The police arrived, followed by an ambulance. They stopped and talked to me a minute, then hurried off to check on Mr. Banning.

I wondered how long I had to wait around.

I wanted to go home now.

I mean, I didn't even want to hunt for the perfect pair of bargain shoes or stop for Ben and Jerry's. That just shows how hard I'd been hit by this.

Anytime a woman passes up Ben and Jerry's or new shoes… well, it's moved beyond a bad day and turned into a found-a-dead-body-on-the-bed sort of day.

I was wondering if I could just sneak out. The authorities had my information already, so they didn't need me. But then *He* walked up to me.

He was tall, lean and oh-so-yummy. Dark hair with just a touch of grey at the temples.

Not one of LA's boy-toys who are a dime a dozen.

No, this was a real man walking toward me like some hero out of a movie.

Maybe he was here to take me away from all this.

Maybe he'd seen me from across the street looking fragile, yet still beautiful.

Okay, so beautiful was a bit unattainable. I'd settle for fragile and cute. Yeah, I could pull off cute on a good day and I felt very, very fragile at the moment.

Ah, my hero.

I sucked in my baby-pooch, pulled out my old acting class skills and concentrated on looking even more fragile and cute. It worked. He walked right up to me, shot me a concerned look, then ... he flashed a badge.

I realized that his concerned look was more of an assessing look.

My hero was a cop.

Okay, so maybe *He* was a cop who was concerned because I looked so fragile?

"Ma'am? You're," he flipped open his little notepad in a very Adam-12 sort of way, and that particular mental-analogy really dated me I realized morosely as he finished, "Quincy Mac?"

"Yes." I thought about fluttering my eyelashes but decided to give up before I embarrassed myself.

"You're the one who found Mr. Banning and called 911?"

"Yes." I wanted to say more, so much more. But even a gorgeous knockout cop couldn't make me forget I'd just found a dead body, at least not for long. And thoughts of Mr. Banning, sitting on his bed, covered in blood with his eyes open, well, that sort of froze the words in my throat.

"The officer over there said that the house has been pretty much wiped clean."

I had professional pride in my job well done. "Not *pretty much*, all the way. Other than the bedroom, which I didn't clean for obvious reasons."

The cop quirked his eyebrow. "He said the bedroom was wiped clean as well."

I think the hunky cop just called me a liar.

Actually, I didn't just think it—I could see it in his eyes. The man actually thought I'd gone into a room with a dead body in it and cleaned it up?

My attraction to him slipped more than just a notch. It evaporated.

"Not by me," I assured him. "I took one look at the body on the bed, called 911 as I got the heck out of there. I guarantee that I didn't stop to clean the room first."

"But you admit you cleaned the rest of the house?" the cop asked.

"Of course I admit it. I'm the maid. That's what they pay me to do. Don't you think that if I'd have known someone had died, I'd have simply called the cops first? If you'd seen what a state the house was in when I arrived, you'd know I'd have welcomed an excuse not to clean it. But I did clean it and I did a fine job of it."

Cleaning houses is an honest profession. I might have been a bit befuddled, but even in my present state I wasn't going to let some cop make me feel less than the professional that I am.

He didn't answer my question. He simply asked, "And the other officers said there were footprints you steamed off the carpet?"

"Yes. I'm good at what I do. When Mac'Cleaners cleans a house, it's totally clean."

"Ma'am, the coroner says that Mr. Banning probably died sometime last night." He paused a moment and sort of gave me a hard stare with his charcoal grey eyes.

That stare did things to me ... my knees felt rather weak and my heart rate sped up. I don't think it was shock.

Lust.

That's what it felt like.

I hadn't had a good case of lust in a while. But I was pretty sure that I remembered how if felt and this was it.

"Quincy," he said, soft and low.

Yes, I wanted to say.

Oh, yes.

I've read that when someone experiences death they want to make love just to prove they're still alive, to prove that they can still feel something.

I think my lust for this cop went deeper than just a need to prove I was alive. It might have been a need to prove I still had a libido, but mainly I think it had something to do with a long, hard orgasm.

I was almost forty and I'd read enough magazine articles to know that meant I was reaching my sexual prime.

Only it had been a long time since I'd been primed.

This guy was making remember how much I enjoyed a good priming.

"Yes," I said out loud. Hoping he'd say, *let's forget about the dead body and get you home to bed.*

Oh, yeah. I wanted him to tuck me in, and then tuck himself right next to me.

Naked.

"Quincy," he said again, "by any chance you have an alibi for last night?"

"An alibi?" I squeaked, all lust-filled thoughts fleeing from my head.

Alibi?

Rats.

I knew what that meant.

I watch *Law and Order*, *Law and Order SVU*, and *Law and Order Criminal Intent*. Is that all? I might be forgetting one, but that's understandable, given my circumstances.

Oh, and I watch *CSI*.

All that television meant I knew that cops didn't ask witnesses for alibis.

They asked suspects for them.

I was a murder suspect.

Continue Reading Steamed: A Maid in LA

ALSO BY HOLLY JACOBS

Romance+ Stories
Just One Thing
Same Time Next Summer
Her Second-Chance Family
Words of the Heart Series
Carry Her Heart
These Three Words
Hold Her Heart

Romantic Comedies
I Waxed My Legs for This?
A Day Late and a Bride Short
Bosom Buddies
Cinderella Wore Tennis Shoes

Cupid Falls
Christmas in Cupid Falls
A Simple Heart: A Cupid Falls Novella

Short Stories and Novellas
Able to Love Again
Labor Day
There He Was
13 Weeks

Nothing But Short Story Series:
Nothing But Love
Nothing But Heart
Nothing But Luck
Rather than buy them individually, try:
Short Stories for the Overworked and Under-Read
Anthology

Maid in LA Series:
My first mystery series!!
Steamed: A Maid in LA Mystery
Dusted: A Maid in LA Mystery
Spruced Up: A Maid in LA Novella
Swept Up: A Maid in LA Mystery
All four books in one edition
Maid in LA Mysteries bundle

Perry Square Series:
Do You Hear What I Hear?
A Day Late and a Bride Short
Dad Today, Groom Tomorrow
Be My Baby
Once Upon a Princess
Once Upon a Prince
Once Upon a King
Here With Me

Everything But ... Series:
Everything But a Groom
Everything But a Bride
Everything But a Wedding
Everything But a Christmas Eve

Everything But a Mother
Everything But a Dog

WLVH Series:
Pickup Lines
Lovehandles
Night Calls
Laugh Lines

Whedon Series:
Unexpected Gifts
A One-of-a-Kind Family
Homecoming Day
A Father's Name

Valley Ridge Series:
You Are Invited... *A Valley Ridge Wedding*
April Showers, *A Valley Ridge Wedding*
A Walk Down the Aisle, *A Valley Ridge Wedding*
A Valley Ridge Christmas